MARJORIE DEAN HIGH SCHOOL JUNIOR

BY

PAULINE LESTER

MARJORIE DEAN HIGH SCHOOL JUNIOR

CHAPTER I—MARJORIE DECLARES HERSELF

"Only to think, next week, at this time, I'll be saying good-bye to you, Mary Raymond." Marjorie Dean's brown eyes rested very wistfully on the sunny-haired girl beside her in the big porch swing.

"You know now, just how dreadfully I felt two years ago when I had to keep thinking about saying good-bye to you," returned Mary in the same wistful intonation. "It was terrible. And after you had gone! Well—it was a good deal worse. Oh, Marjorie, I wish I could live this last year over again. If only——"

Marjorie laid light fingers on Mary's lips. "You mustn't speak of some things, Lieutenant," she said quickly. "If you do I won't listen. Forget everything except the wonderful summer we've had together."

Mary caught the soft little hand in both hers. "It has been wonderful," she agreed rather unsteadily. "I'll have the memory of it to treasure when I'm away off in Colorado. I can't believe that I am really going so far away from you. I hope I'll like the West. Next summer you must come out there and visit me, Marjorie. By that time I'll be a little bit at home in such a strange, new country."

"I'd love to do that," responded Marjorie with an eagerness that merged almost immediately again into regretful reflection.

A sad little silence fell upon the two in the porch swing. Each young heart was heavy with dread of the coming separation. This was the second time in two years that the call to say farewell had sounded for Marjorie Dean and Mary Raymond.

Those who have followed Marjorie Dean through her freshman and sophomore years at high school are already familiar with the details of Mary's and Marjorie's first separation. In "Marjorie Dean, High School Freshman," was recorded the story of the way in which Marjorie had come to leave her chum at the beginning of their first year in Franklin High School, in the city of B——, to take up her residence in the far-off town of Sanford, there to become a freshman at Sanford High. In her new home she had made many friends, chief among them Constance Stevens, to whom she had been greatly drawn by reason of a strong resemblance between Constance and Mary. In an earnest endeavor to bring sunshine to the former's poverty-stricken lot she had thereby involved herself in a series of school-girl difficulties, which followed her throughout the year. True to herself, Marjorie met them bravely and conquered them, one by one, proving herself a staunch follower of the high code of honor she had adopted for her own.

With the advent of Mary Raymond into her home for a year's stay, Marjorie was confronted by a new and painful problem. "Marjorie Dean, High School Sophomore," found Marjorie enmeshed in the tangled web which Mary's jealousy of Constance Stevens wove about the three girls. Led into bitter doubt of Marjorie by Mignon La Salle, a mischief-making French girl who had made Marjorie's freshman days miserable, Mary Raymond had been guilty of a disloyalty, which had come near to estranging the two girls forever. It was not until their sophomore year was almost over that an awakening had come to Mary, and with it an earnest repentance, which led to equity and peace.

It was to this which Mary had been about to refer mournfully when Marjorie's gentle hand had sealed her repentant utterance. All that summer the two girls had been earnestly engaged in trying to make up for those lost days. Constance and Mary were now on the most friendly terms. The three had spent an ideal month together at the seashore, with no hateful shadow to darken the pleasure of that delightful outing. Later Constance had left them to spend the remainder of her vacation with her family in the mountains. The Deans had lingered in their seaside cottage until the last of August. Now September had arrived, her hazy hints of coming Autumn reminding the world at large that their summer playtime was over.

To Mary Raymond it was a pertinent reminder that her days under the Deans' hospitable canopy were numbered. In fact, only seven of them remained. On the next Friday morning she would say her last farewells to speed away to Denver, Colorado, where, on her invalid mother's account, the Raymonds were to make their home. So it is scarcely to be wondered at that Marjorie and Mary were decidedly melancholy, as they sat hand in hand, bravely trying to meet the trial which lay before them.

"I wonder if Jerry will come home to-day." Marjorie rose from the swing with an abruptness that set it to swaying gently. The weight of parting had grown heavier during that brief silence and she was very near to tears.

"I don't know. Her letter said Thursday or Friday, didn't it?" Mary's voice shook slightly. She, too, was on the verge of a breakdown.

"Yes." Marjorie's back was toward Mary as she answered. She walked to the end of the spacious veranda and gazed down the pebbled drive. Just then she felt as though the sight of Geraldine Macy's round, good-humored face would be most welcome. Slowly returning to where Mary still sat, she said: "As this is Friday, Jerry will surely——"

"Marjorie!" called a clear voice from within the house. "The telephone is ringing."

"Coming, Captain!" Marjorie quickened to sudden action. "I hope it's Jerry," she flung over her shoulder as she ran to the open door. "Come on, Mary."

Mary needed no second invitation. By the time Marjorie had reached the telephone, she was only a step behind her chum.

"Hello! Yes, this is Marjorie. Oh, Jerry!" Marjorie gave a little squeal of delight. "We were just talking of you. We wondered if you'd be home to-day. Won't you come over now? You will? Well, then, hurry as fast as ever you can. We're crazy to see you. Mary wants to talk to you. Just say 'hello' to her and hang up the receiver." Marjorie cast a playful glance at the girl beside her. "You can talk to her when you get here."

Marjorie held the receiver toward Mary, who greeted Jerry in brief but affectionate fashion and obediently hung up. "Always do as your superior officer tells you," she commented with a smile.

"That's pure sarcasm," retorted Marjorie gaily. "The question is, am I your superior officer or are you mine? This business of both being lieutenants has its drawbacks. We can never know just who's who."

"I ought to be second lieutenant and you first," demurred Mary soberly. "I didn't deserve to become a first with you last June after——"

"Mary!" Marjorie cried out in distressed concern. Her brown eyes were filled with tender reproach. "Aren't you ever going to forget?"

"I can't." Mary turned her face half away, then the flood of sadness she had been fighting back all afternoon overtook her. Stumbling to the stairs she sat down on the lowest step, her face hidden in her hands, her shoulders shaking.

"Poor, dear Lieutenant." Her own eyes overflowing, Marjorie dropped down beside Mary and wound her arms about the dejected figure.

"This is a nice reception! I see I shall have to welcome myself. Why, how are you, Geraldine? Boo, hoo! It's a wonder you wouldn't ring. You never did have any manners. I don't see why you called, anyway. Boo, hoo!"

The first sound of a loud, cheerful voice brought the weepers to their feet. A loud, anguished "Boo, hoo!" sent them into half-tearful giggles.

"That's more like it," approved the stout girl in the doorway, her round face alive with kindly solicitude. "If I had sensitive feelings I might think you were crying because you'd invited me to call. But I haven't. Hal says I am the most unfeeling person he knows. He only says that when his little sister can't see things the way he does."

Jerry rattled off these pleasantries while in the midst of a rapturous embrace, bestowed upon her plump person by two now broadly-smiling mourners.

"It's splendid to see you again, Jerry," caroled Marjorie, hugging her friend with bearish enthusiasm. Mary echoed Marjorie's fervent greeting.

"The mere sight of me is always inspiring," grinned Jerry, winding an arm about each friend. "I hope you have both noticed by this time that I am a great deal thinner than I was last June. I've lost two pounds. Isn't that some loss?"

"Perfectly remarkable," agreed Marjorie mischievously. "Come on out on the veranda, Jerry. We have such a lot to talk about."

Four determined, affectionate arms propelled Jerry to the wide, vine-decked porch, established her in the big porch swing, and climbed in beside her.

"Now, tell me, children, why these weeps?" Jerry demanded practically, still retaining her loving hold of her two friends.

"They've been on the way all day," confessed Marjorie. "We've both tried not to cry, but—somehow——" Her voice faltered. "You see, Jerry, this is Mary's and my last week together. Mary's going away off to Colorado next week."

"You don't mean it?" Jerry sat up very straight, looking wide-eyed concern. "You never said a thing about it in your letter. I mean letters. I believe you did write me two." Jerry registered comical accusation.

"Don't remind me of my sins of omission," Marjorie laughed, flushing a trifle. "I always mean to write, but somehow I never do. We didn't know until the week before we came from the seashore that Mary would have to go so soon. We thought it wouldn't be until November." Again her tones quavered suspiciously.

"I see." Jerry frowned to hide her own inclination to mourn. During the brief time they were thrown together, after the reunion of Marjorie and Mary, she had learned to know and love the real Mary Raymond. "I'm more sorry than I can say. I thought we'd all be together for our junior year at Sanford High."

"Of course, I am anxious to be with mother and father," put in Mary loyally, "but I hate to leave Sanford. There are lots of things I meant to do this year that I didn't do last year."

"But you can't be in two places at once," was Jerry's blunt consolation. "Never mind, Mary, you can come back to visit us and we'll write you lots of letters. Marjorie is such a splendid correspondent." Her accompanying jolly chuckle robbed this last pertinent fling of offence. "We'll write you all the news. That reminds me, I've some for you girls. You'll never guess who stayed at the same hotel with us this summer. I didn't write about it, because I wanted to have it to tell when I came home."

Mary cast a sidelong glance at the stout girl. There had been a faint touch of disgust in Jerry's intonation. "Was it—Mignon?" she asked, half hesitant.

"Right you are. How did you guess it?"

"Oh, I just wondered," was Mary's brief response. A tide of red had risen to her white skin, called there by distressing memories.

"Yes, it was our dear Mignon," continued Jerry briskly. "And she has a friend, Rowena Farnham, who likewise stayed at our hotel. Believe me, they were a well-matched pair. You see the La Salles usually go to Severn Beach every summer, but they always stay at Cliff House. We always go to the Sea Gull. That's the whole length of the beach from their hotel. Imagine how pleased I was to see Mignon come parading down to dinner one evening, after we'd been there about two weeks. I was so disgusted that I wanted my father to pack up and move us over to Cliff House. But he wouldn't, the hard-hearted person.

"That is only part of my tale. The worst now comes trailing along. It's about this Rowena Farnham. It seems that the Farnhams moved to Sanford last June just after school closed and——"

"Is this Rowena Farnham a very tall, pretty girl with perfectly gorgeous auburn hair and big black eyes?" broke in Mary abruptly.

"Yes. Where did you ever see her?" demanded Jerry. "Where was I that I didn't?"

"Oh, I saw her one day in the post-office with Mignon. It was after you had gone away. I thought she must be a guest at the La Salles'."

"You thought wrong. She lives in that big house with the immense grounds just the other side of the La Salles' home. It's the one with that terribly high, ornamental iron fence. I always used to call it the Jail. It made me think of one. But that's not my news, either. This new girl is going to be a sophomore at Sanford High. I'm sorry for poor old Sanford High."

"Why?" A curious note of alarm sprang into Marjorie's question. After two stormy years at high school, she longed for uneventful peace. Jerry's emphatic grumble came like a far-off roll of thunder, prophesying storm.

"Why?" Jerry warmed to her subject. "Because she is a terror. I can see it in her eye. Just now she and Mignon are as chummy as can be. If they stay chummy, look out for trouble. If they don't, look out for more trouble."

"Perhaps you may find this new girl quite different," suggested Mary hopefully. "It's not fair to judge her by Mignon. Very likely she hasn't any idea that—that——" She was thinking of how completely she had once fallen under Mignon's spell.

"That Mignon is Mignon, you mean," interrupted Jerry. "She ought to know her after being with her all summer. I'll bet she does. That's just why I think she's a trouble-maker. They always hang together, you know."

Marjorie slipped from the swing and faced her friends with the air of one who has suddenly arrived at a definite conclusion. For a moment she stood regarding Jerry in silence, hands clasped behind her back.

"There's just one thing about it, Jerry," she began firmly, "and that is: I will not have my junior year spoiled by Mignon La Salle or her friends. Last year we tried to help Mignon and our plan didn't work. I thought once that she had a better self, but now it would take a good deal to make me believe it. She caused me a great deal of unnecessary unhappiness and she almost made Constance lose her part in the operetta. And little Charlie! I can't forgive her for the way she treated that baby. This year I am going to go on with my school just as though I had never known her. I hope I won't have to play on the same basket ball team with her or against any team that she plays on. I've had enough of Mignon La Salle. I'm going to steer clear of her."

CHAPTER II—ALL IN HONOR OF MARY

"Be sure not to pack your white lace dress, Lieutenant." Marjorie delivered this reminder from the open doorway of the pretty blue room which Mary had so long regarded as her own special nook.

From a kneeling position before her trunk Mary Raymond turned her head, her eyes two mournful blue stars. "It's over there," she returned, nodding somberly toward the bed. "Everything else that had to be packed is packed. I can put my dress in the last thing to-night. I'm so glad Connie is home in time to see me off on my journey. I hope she and Charlie will come over early this afternoon."

"They will." The blithe assurance held a significance which Mary did not catch. The shadow of the coming separation now hung more heavily upon her. Marjorie's cheery reply caused her to wonder vaguely if her chum would really miss her so very much. The next instant she put the thought away from her as unworthy. Of course Marjorie would miss her. Still she could scarcely be blamed if she did not. In spite of the long, happy summer they had spent together, occasionally the past rose to torture Mary.

Packing her effects had been a severe trial. Everything she touched called forth memories. There was the blue linen frock she had worn on the morning of her first entrance into Sanford High School. The very sight of it filled her with remorse. And the dress she had worn on Christmas Day, when the merciful Flag of Truce had bade a halt to the hostilities which her own unreasonable jealousy had created. More than one tear had fallen on the various dainty articles of wearing apparel as she consigned them to her trunk. She wished above all to be brave and cheerful, even to the very moment of farewell, but she found it hard to fight back the terrible feeling of oppression that clutched at her heart.

From her position in the doorway, Marjorie had watched Mary for a moment or two before speaking. She had guessed that the work of packing would be something of a dolorous labor, which Mary might prefer to perform alone. At heart she, too, was sad, but in her mind lurked a pleasant knowledge which for the present Mary did not share. It was this particular bit of knowledge that made it difficult for her to keep a sober face as she met Mary's doleful gaze.

"I'm going to wear white, too," she said brightly. "Captain finished my new lingerie frock yesterday. As long as you're through packing, why not get dressed for dinner now? I'm going to, even if it is only three o'clock. Then when Connie and Charlie come we can take a stroll down to Sargent's. That is, if we care to." Again her lovely face threatened to break forth into the smiles.

"All right." Mary's acquiescence came rather listlessly. Rising from the floor she began somewhat spiritless preparations toward making ready to receive the expected guests.

"I'm going to my house now to put on my costliest raiment." Flashing a mischievous glance toward Mary, Marjorie disappeared from the doorway and tripped down the hall. Once inside her "house," as she had whimsically named her pink and white room, she executed a gleeful little dance for her own benefit. "She doesn't suspect a thing," was her jubilant comment.

But while the two girls were engaged in arraying themselves to do honor to Constance, a most peculiar state of affairs was in progress downstairs. Through the wide flung hall door, one after another flitted a mysterious procession of girls, moving with the noiseless tread of a flock of ghosts. Their bright-eyed, smiling faces and gala attire, however, marked them as being particularly human. One of the seven specters bore a strong resemblance to Mary herself, and the diminutive black-eyed sprite she led by the hand seemed on the verge of breaking forth into an ecstatic flow of joyful sounds.

Apparently, Mrs. Dean had also been suddenly bereft of speech. Only her twinkling eyes and smiling lips gave sign of just how greatly welcome were her silent guests. Ushering them into the living room she nodded brightly, laid a warning finger to her lips and softly withdrew, pulling together the silken portieres. A half-smothered giggle, to which no self-respecting ghost would have stooped to give utterance, followed her. Then profound stillness reigned within.

"Are you ready, Mary?" A bewitching, brown-eyed vision in white pranced in upon Mary as she was slowly adjusting the soft loops of her wide, white ribbon sash. "Let me tie your sash." Marjorie's nimble fingers set themselves to work. "There you are. You do look so perfectly sweet in white. Now smile and say prettily, 'Thank you for them kind words, Miss Marjorie.' That's what Delia always says when she dresses up and I tell her how fine she looks."

Marjorie's buoyant spirits were so irresistible as to bring the coveted light into Mary's mournful eyes. "Forward, march! Here we go." Seizing Mary gently by the shoulders she marched her down the hall to the stairway. "Break ranks," she ordered. "The gallant regiment can't afford to tumble downstairs."

"Halt!" came the order, as Mary reached the lower hall a step ahead of her commander. "We will now make an invasion on the living room. Two's right, march!"

Mary obediently marched. Of her own accord she came to an abrupt halt. "Oh!" she gasped. Her amazed exclamation was drowned in a chorus of gleeful shouts as seven very lively apparitions closed in around her.

"Charlie never said a word!" shrieked a high, triumphant voice. "We comed to see you. Hooray!" A small, joyful figure hurled itself straight into Mary's arms. She stooped and hugged him close, her golden head bent to the youngster's. Straightening, she glimpsed the affectionate circle of girls through a mist of unbidden tears. "I'm so glad and so surprised to see all of you," she faltered. "And you knew it all the time!" She caught Marjorie's hand.

"Of course I knew it. Now we are even. You gave me a surprise party once, so I thought I'd return the compliment," laughed Marjorie. "I could hardly keep it to myself, though. Every time I looked at you I wanted to say, 'Cheer up, the best is yet to come.'"

"It's a good thing it wasn't long coming," retorted Jerry Macy. "I never knew how much I liked to talk until I had to keep still."

"You must have slipped into the house like shadows," declared Mary happily. Her sad expression had quite vanished with the unexpected honor that had been done her. She felt that, after all, she held some small place in the affections of Marjorie's intimate friends, and the cloud of doubt that had obsessed her rolled away.

"We did do that arriving stunt rather well," was Harriet Delaney's complacent comment. "Of course, Susie giggled. We expected she would, though. The rest of us were above reproach."

"No wonder I giggled," defended Susan Atwell. "If you had been the last one in line you'd have laughed, too. You girls looked as if you were trying to walk on eggshells, and when Jerry crossed the room in about three steps, it was too much for me." Susan's cheerful chuckle broke forth anew and went the rounds.

"Well, children, what is your pleasure?" inquired Marjorie. "Shall we stay here, or sit on the veranda, or establish ourselves in the pagoda, or what?"

"The pagoda for mine," decided Jerry, "provided the rest of you are of the same mind. We can sit in a circle and tell sad stories of the deaths of kings, etc. All those in favor of this lively pastime please say 'Aye;' contrary, keep quiet."

"Aye," came the willing response.

"What for is 'Aye?'" calmly demanded Charlie Stevens of Mary, to whom he had immediately attached himself.

"Oh, it means that Charlie can go out with us to the summer house and have a nice time, if he would like to," explained Mary.

"Charlie don't want to," was the frank response. "Where's Delia?" Fond recollections of frequent visits to the Dean kitchen, invariably productive of toothsome gifts, lurked in the foreground. "Delia likes to see me."

"You mean you like to see Delia," laughed Constance. "But you know you came to see Mrs. Dean and Marjorie and Mary," she reminded.

"I've seen them. Now I have to see Delia."

"Delia wins the day," smiled Mrs. Dean. "You are all jilted. Very well, Charlie, you and I will pay our respects to Delia. Come on." She stretched forth an inviting hand to the little boy, who accepted it joyfully, and trotted off with her to invade good-natured Delia's domain.

"As long as our one cavalier has been lured away from us by Delia we might as well try to console one another," laughed Marjorie.

"He's growing terribly spoiled," apologized Constance. "My aunt adores him and thinks he must have everything he asks for. He's a good little boy, though, in spite of all the petting he gets."

"He's a perfect darling," dimpled Susan Atwell. "He says such quaint, funny things. Has he ever tried to run away since the night of the operetta?"

"No." Constance made brief reply. Her gaze wandered to Mary Raymond, who was talking busily with Harriet Delaney and Esther Lind. The vision of a fair-haired, blue-eyed girl, leading a small runaway up to the stage door of the theatre rose before her. Next to Marjorie Dean, Mary ranked second in her heart. Constance felt suddenly very humble in the possession of two such wonderful friends. Life had been kinder to her than she deserved was her grateful thought.

Susan eyed her curiously. Although she was very fond of Constance, she did not in the least understand her. Now she said rather timidly, "I hope you didn't mind because I spoke of the operetta and Charlie's running away, Connie?"

Constance promptly came out of her day-dream. "You brought it all back to me," she smiled. "I was just wondering what I'd ever done to deserve such friends as I've made here in Sanford. I can't bear to think that Mary won't be with us this year."

Before Susan could reply, Jerry interrupted them with, "Come along, girls. The sooner we get settled the longer we'll have to talk."

It was a merry, light-hearted band that strolled out of the house and across the lawn to the honeysuckle-draped pagoda, situated at the far end of the velvety stretch of green. Mary and Marjorie brought up the rear, their arms piled high with bright-hued cushions, and the guests soon disposed themselves on the bench built circular fashion around the pagoda, or sought the comfort of the several wicker chairs.

Brought together again after more than two months' separation, a busy wagging of tongues was in order, mingled with the ready laughter that high-spirited youth alone knows. Everyone had something interesting to tell of her vacation and rejoiced accordingly in the telling. Father Time flew in his fleetest fashion, but no one of the group paid the slightest attention to the fact. From vacation, the conversation gradually drifted into school channels and a lively discussion of junior plans ensued.

"By the way, girls," remarked Jerry Macy with the careless assumption of casualty which was her favorite method of procedure when about to retail some amazing bit of news. "Did you know that Miss Archer almost decided to resign her position at Sanford High for one in Chicago?"

"Of course we didn't know it, and you know we didn't," laughed Susan Atwell. "Whenever Jerry begins with 'By the way,' and tries to look innocent you may know she has something startling to offer."

"Where on earth do you pick up all your news, Jerry?" asked Constance Stevens. "You always seem to know everything about everybody."

"Oh, it just happens to come my way," grinned Jerry. "I heard about Miss Archer from my father. He's just been elected to the Board of Education."

"She isn't really going to leave Sanford High, is she, Jerry?" An anxious frown puckered Marjorie's smooth forehead. She hated to think of high school without Miss Archer.

"No. At first she thought she would, but afterward she decided that she'd rather stay here. She told father that she had grown so fond of the dear old school she couldn't bear to leave it. I'm certainly glad she's not going to resign. If she did we might have kind, delightful Miss Merton for a principal. Then—good night!" Jerry relapsed into slang to emphasize her disgust of such a possibility.

"I shouldn't like that," Marjorie remarked bluntly. "Still, I can't help feeling a little bit sorry for Miss Merton. She shuts out all the bright, pleasant things in life and just sticks to the disagreeable ones. Sometimes I wonder if she was ever young or had ever been happy."

"She's been a regular Siberian crab-apple ever since I can remember," grumbled Jerry. "Why, when I was a kidlet in knee skirts she was the terror of Sanford High. I guess she must have been crossed in love about a hundred years ago." Jerry giggled a trifle wickedly.

"She was," affirmed quiet Irma with a smile, "but not a hundred years ago. I never knew it until this summer."

"Here is something I don't seem to know about," satirized Jerry. "How did that happen, I wonder?"

"Don't keep us in suspense, Irma," implored Muriel Harding. "If Miss Merton ever had a love affair it's your duty to tell us about it. I can't imagine such an impossibility. Did it happen here in Sanford? How did you come to hear of it?"

A circle of eager faces were turned expectantly toward Irma. "My aunt, whom I visited this summer, told me about it," she began. "She lived in Sanford when she was a girl and knew Miss Merton then. They went to school together. There were no high schools then; just an academy for young men and women. Miss Merton was really a pretty girl. She had pink cheeks and bright eyes and beautiful, heavy, dark hair. She had a sister, too, who wasn't a bit pretty.

"They were very quiet girls who hardly ever went to parties and never paid much attention to the boys they knew in Sanford. When Miss Merton was about eighteen and her sister twenty-one, a handsome young naval officer came to visit some friends in Sanford on a furlough. He was introduced to both sisters, and called on them two or three times. They lived with their father in that little house on Sycamore Street where Miss Merton still lives. The young ensign's furlough was nearly over when he met them, so he didn't have much time to get well acquainted with them. The night before he went away he asked Miss Merton if he might write to her and she said 'Yes.'"

"Some story," cut in Jerry. "And did he write?"

"Don't interrupt me, Jeremiah," reproved Irma. "Yes, he wrote, but——"

"Miss Merton never got the letter," supplemented the irrepressible Jerry. "That's the way it always happens in books."

"All right. You may tell the rest of it," teased Irma, her eyes twinkling.

"Someone please smother Jerry's head in a sofa cushion, so she can't interrupt," pleaded Harriet.

"Try it," challenged Jerry. "Excuse me, Irma. I solemnly promise to behave like a clam. On with the miraculous, marvelous memoirs of meritorious Miss Merton."

"Where was I? Oh, yes. The young ensign wrote, as he thought, to Miss Merton, but in some way he had confused the two sisters' first names. So he wrote to Alice Merton, her sister, instead, thinking it was our Miss Merton."

"How awful! The very idea! What a dreadful mistake!" came from the highly interested listeners.

"The sister was delighted because she liked the ensign a lot and thought he didn't care much about her. You can imagine how Miss Merton felt. She never said a word to anyone then about his asking her if he might write. She thought he had just been flirting with her when really he had fallen in love with her. Then his ship went on a trip around the world, but he kept on writing to the sister, and at last he asked her to marry him. So they were engaged and he sent her a beautiful diamond ring. They planned to be married when he received his next furlough. But when he came to Sanford to claim his bride, he found that he had made a terrible mistake."

"What did he do then?" chorused half a dozen awed voices.

"Oh, he made the best of it and married the sister," Irma replied with a shrug. "I suppose he felt that he couldn't very well do anything else. Perhaps he didn't have the courage to. But one day before his wedding he went to the house and found Miss Merton alone. She had been crying and he felt so sorry that he tried to find out what was the matter. Somehow they came to an understanding, but it was too late. Three or four years after that he was drowned during a storm at sea. Miss Merton never quite got over it all, and it changed her disposition, I guess."

"What a sad story." Constance Stevens' blue eyes were soft with sympathy.

"That makes Miss Merton seem like a different person, doesn't it?" Marjorie thoughtfully knitted her brows.

"I suppose that is why she acts as though she hated young people," offered Mary. "We probably remind her of her cheated youth."

"She should have been particular enough to let that stupid ensign know that she was she," criticized practical Jerry. "I'm glad I haven't a sister. There's no danger of any future aspirant for my hand and heart getting me mixed with Hal."

The sentimental shadow cast upon the group by Irma's romantic tale disappeared in a gale of laughter.

"Honestly, Jerry Macy, you haven't the least idea of romance," giggled Susan. "Here Irma tells us a real love story and you spoil it all about a minute afterward."

"Can't help it," asserted Jerry stoutly. "I have to say what I think."

"Oh, here come Captain and Charlie," cried Marjorie, sighting a gracious figure in white descending the steps with Charlie in tow. "That means dinner is about to be served, children. Our farewell feast to Lieutenant Mary Raymond."

CHAPTER III—THE SHIELD OF VALOR

A chorus of ohs and ahs ascended as the guests filed into a dining room, the decoration of which spelled Patriotism in large capitals. In honor of the pretty soldier play to which she and Mary had so long clung, Marjorie had decreed that the dinner should be a patriotic affair so far as decorations went. The walls of the large, attractive room were plentifully festooned with red, white and blue bunting. Flags were in evidence everywhere. From the center of the large oak table a large doll dressed as Uncle Sam held gallantly aloft the tri-colored ribbons that extended to each place. On one side of him stood a smaller doll dressed in the khaki uniform of the United States soldier. On the other, a valiant Jackie stood guard. At each cover was a small soldier doll and the place cards were tiny, folded, silk flags, each guest's name written in one of the stripes of white uppermost.

Mary occupied the seat of honor at the head of the table, with Marjorie at her right and Constance at her left. But at the departing Lieutenant's place rose an amazing pile of tissue-paper wrapped, beribboned bundles that smacked of Christmas.

"Company, attention," called Mrs. Dean from the foot of the table, the instant the party had seated themselves. "Lieutenant Raymond, you are ordered to inspect your wealth before mess."

"I—oh——" stammered the abashed Lieutenant, regarding said "wealth" in stupefaction. "All those things are not really for me!"

"Open them and see," directed Marjorie, her face radiant with unselfish happiness. "Every one of them holds an original poetic message. None of us knows what the other wrote. You are to read them in a loud voice and satisfy our curiosity. Now hurry up and begin."

Under a battery of smiling faces, Mary slowly undid a good-sized square bundle. With slightly shaking fingers she drew forth a white box. When opened it displayed several sizes of note paper and envelopes bearing her monogram in silver. Picking up a card she steadied her voice and read:

"You say, of course, 'I'll surely write,'

But when you've traveled out of sight,

This nice white box may then remind you

Of Jerry Macy, far behind you."

"I truly will write you, Jerry. Thank you." Mary beamed affectionately on the stout girl. "It's a lovely present, and my own monogram, too."

"See that you do," nodded Jerry gruffly. She loved to give, but she did not relish being thanked.

"Next," smilingly ordered Marjorie. "If you don't hurry and open them, we shall all starve."

The next package disclosed a dainty little leather combination purse and vanity case from Muriel Harding with the succinct advice:

> "Don't lose your ticket or your money,
>
> To be stone broke is far from funny.
>
> When wicked cinders seek your eye,
>
> Consult your mirror on the sly."

After Muriel had been thanked and her practical, poetic advice lauded, Mary went on with her delightful investigation. An oblong bundle turned out to be a box of nut chocolates from Susan, who offered:

> "In time of homesick tribulation,
>
> Turn to this toothsome consolation.
>
> To eat it up will be amusin'——
>
> Here's sweet farewell from giggling Susan."

"Giggling Susan's" effort brought forth a ripple of giggles from all sides.

"That's my present," squealed Charlie, as Mary fingered a tiny package ornamented with a huge red bow. "It's a——"

"Shh!" warned Constance, placing prompt fingers on the too-willing lips.

Mary cast the child a tender glance as she glimpsed a tiny leather violin case, partially obscured by a card. In this instance it was Uncle John Roland who had played poet, after receiving Charlie's somewhat garbled instructions regarding the sentiment.

"Say it s'loud as you can," commanded the excited youngster.

Mary complied, reading in a purposely loud tone that must have been intensely gratifying to the diminutive giver:

> "Once when away from home I ranned
>
> To play my fiddle in the band,
>
> You comed and finded me, 'n then
>
> I never ranned away again.
>
> So now I'm always nice and good
>
> An' do as Connie says I should,
>
> And 'cause you're going to run away
>
> You'd better write to me some day!
>
> Inside the little fiddle box
>
> There is a fountain pen that talks
>
> On paper—it's for you from me,
>
> The great musishun; your friend, C."

As Mary read the last line she slipped from her place to Charlie and kissed the gleeful, upturned face. "You darling boy," she quavered. "Mary won't forget to write."

"Mine's the best of all," observed Charlie with modest frankness, as he enthusiastically returned the kiss.

Back in her place again, Mary finished the affectionate inspection of the tokens her friends had taken so much pleasure in giving. There was a book from Harriet, a folded metal drinking cup in a leather case from Esther Lind, a hand-embroidered pin and needle case from Irma, a pair of soft, dark-blue leather slippers from Constance, and a wonderful Japanese silk kimono from Mrs. Dean. The remembrances had all been selected as first aids to Mary during her long journey across the country. With each one went a humorous verse, composed with more or less effort on the part of the givers.

But one package now remained to be opened. Its diminutive size and shape hinted that it might have come from the jeweler's. Mary knew it to be Marjorie's farewell token to her. She would have liked to examine it in private. She was almost sure that she was going to cry. She thrust back the inclination, however, flashing a tender, wavering smile at her chum as she untied the silver cord that bound the box. It bore the name of a Sanford jeweler and when the lid was off revealed a round, gold monogrammed locket, gleaming dully against its pale blue silk bed. In a tiny circular groove of the box was a fine-grained gold chain.

Mary's changeful face registered many emotions as she took the locket in her hands and stared at it in silence. Acting on a swift, overwhelming impulse she sprang mutely from her chair and rushed out of the room. Marjorie half rose from her place, then sat down again. "Lieutenant will come back soon," she said fondly. "She hasn't really deserted from the army, she's only taken a tiny leave of absence. I remember just how I felt when some of the boys and girls of Franklin High gave me a surprise party. That was the night this came to me." She patted the butterfly pin that had figured so prominently in her freshman year at Sanford. "I almost cried like a baby. I remember that the whole table blurred while Mary was making a speech to me about my beautiful pin." Marjorie talked on with the kindly object of centering the guests' attention on herself until Mary should return.

Meanwhile, in the living room Mary Raymond was engaged in the double task of trying to suppress her tears and open the locket at the same time. Her eyes brimming, she worked at the refractory gold catch with insistent fingers. Opened at last, she beheld Marjorie's lovely face smiling out at her. On the inside of the upper half of the locket was engraved, "Mary from Marjorie." Below was the beautiful Spanish phrase, "Para siempre," literally translated, "for always," but meaning "forever."

Within a brief space of time, following her flight, the runaway reappeared, her eyelids slightly pink. "I hope you will all pardon me," she apologized prettily. "I—I—couldn't help it. You've been so sweet to me. I can't ever thank you as you deserve to be thanked for giving me so many lovely things; the very ones I shall need most when I'm traveling. I am sure you must know how dear you all are to me; dearer even than my Franklin High friends. I hope each one of you will write to me. I'll truly try hard not only to be a good correspondent, but always to be worthy of your friendship."

Mary's earnest words met ready responses of good fellowship from those whom she had once scorned. Everything was so different now. The new Mary Raymond was an entire opposite to the sullen-faced young person who had once flouted all overtures of friendship on the part of Marjorie's particular cronies. Beyond an eloquent hand clasp and, "My picture locket is wonderful, Lieutenant. Thank you over and over," Mary had reserved further expression of her appreciation until the two chums should be entirely by themselves.

The delightful dinner ended with a general distribution of fancy cracker bon-bons, which the guests snapped open with a will, to find cunning caps representing the flags of various nations. They donned these with alacrity and trooped into the living room for an evening of stunts in which music played an important part. Constance lifted up her exquisite voice untiringly, weaving her magic spell about her eager listeners. Jerry sang a comic song, mostly off the key, merely to prove the impossibility of her vocal powers. Charlie Stevens, who had trustfully tugged his faithful fiddle along, insisted on rendering a solo of anguishing shrieks and squawks, assuming the majestic mien of a virtuoso. He took himself so seriously that no one dared laugh, although the desire to do so was throttled with difficulty. Susan was prevailed upon to perform a scarf dance, her one accomplishment, using a strip of red, white and blue bunting with graceful effect. Harriet Delaney also sang a ballad, and Esther Lind offered a beautiful Swedish folk song she had learned from her father, who had sung it as a boy in far-off Scandinavia. When the small repertoire of soloists had been exhausted, everyone turned to with Constance at the piano, and made the living room ring with school songs.

Just before the farewell party broke up the door bell rang. Its loud, insistent peal brought a significant exchange of glances, in which Mary alone did not share. Mrs. Dean hurried into the hall. A moment and she returned to the living room, escorting Delia, whose broad, homely face was wreathed in smiles. She advanced toward Mary, holding out a goodly sheaf of letters. "Special delivery, Miss Mary," she announced. "May yez have many of the same." She made a little bobbing bow as Mary took them, bestowed a friendly grin on the company and waddled out.

"I don't understand." Mary seemed overcome by this fresh surprise. "Are they all for me?"

"They're your railway comforts, Lieutenant," laughed Marjorie. "There's a letter from each of us. You can read one a day. There are enough to reach to Denver and a few thrown in to cure the blues after you get there. So you see we won't let you forget us."

"It's the nicest reminder I could possibly have. I don't need a single thing to make me remember you, though. You're all here in my heart to stay as long as I live." Mary had never appeared more sweetly appealing than she now looked, as her clear tones voiced her inner sentiments.

"You're a nice girl," approved Charlie Stevens. "If I ever grow to be's tall's you, Mary Raymond, I'll be married to you and you can play in the band, too. Uncle John'll buy you a fiddle."

This calm disposal of Mary's future drove sentiment to the winds. Unconsciously, little Charlie had sounded a merry note just in time to lift the pall which is always bound to hang over a company devoted to the saying of farewells.

At eleven o'clock Mary and Marjorie accompanied their guests to the gate, the latter avowing their intention to be at the station the following morning to see Mary off on her journey. The two girls strolled back to the house, under the stars, their arms entwined about each other's waists.

"We had a beautiful evening, Lieutenant. How I wish General could have been here. I hate to go away without saying good-bye to him," sighed Mary.

"I'm sorry, too. I wish he could always be at home. He has to be away from Sanford and home so much." Marjorie echoed Mary's sigh. Brightening, she said: "I've another dear surprise for you, though. Come up to my house and I'll give it to you. It's his farewell message. He wanted you to have it the very last thing to-night."

"We are going upstairs, Captain," called Mary, as they passed through the living room. "Want to come?"

"Later," returned Mrs. Dean. She was too good a commander to intrude upon the last precious moments of confidence her little army still had left to them.

Marjorie marched Mary to the pink and white window seat and playfully ordered, "Sit down and fold your hands like a nice, obedient lieutenant. Shut your eyes and don't open them until I say so."

Tripping gleefully to the chiffonier she opened the top drawer, bringing forth a small package and a square white envelope. Tucking them into Mary's folded hands she said, "First you may open your eyes; then you must open your presents. I haven't the least idea what's in the package or what the letter says. General mailed them to me from Boston."

Two pairs of eyes, bright with affectionate curiosity, bent themselves eagerly on the little quaintly enameled box, which Mary hastily unwrapped. "Oh!" was the concerted exclamation. On a white satin pad lay an exquisitely dainty gold pin. It was in the form of a shield. Across the top winked three small jewels set in a row, a ruby, a diamond and a sapphire.

"'Three cheers for the red, white and blue,'" sang Marjorie, dropping down beside Mary and hugging her enthusiastically. "Do read the letter,

Lieutenant. We'll rave about this cunning pin afterward. Oh, I forgot. Perhaps General didn't mean me to know what he wrote."

"Of course he did," flung back Mary loyally. "We'll read it together." Tearing open the envelope, she unfolded the letter and read aloud:

"Beloved Lieutenant:

"You are going away to a far country on a long hike, and, as it is the duty of every good general to look to the welfare of his soldiers, I am sending you the magic Shield of Valor to protect you in time of need. It is a token of honor for a brave lieutenant who fought a memorable battle and won the victory against heavy odds. It is a magic shield, in that it offers protection only to the soldier who has met and worsted the giant, Self. It was wrought from the priceless metal of Golden Deeds and set with the eyes of Endurance, Truth and Constancy. No enemy, however deadly, can prevail against it. It is a talisman, the wearing of which must bring Honor and Peace.

"Dear little comrade, may happiness visit you in your new barracks. Let the bugle call 'On duty' find you marching head up, colors flying, until 'Taps' sounds at the close of each busy day. Though you have answered the call to a new post, your general hopes with all his heart that you will some day hurry back to your regiment in Sanford to receive the sword of captaincy and the enthusiastic welcome of your brother officers. May all good go with you.

"Loyally,

"General Dean."

Mary's voice trailed away into a silence that outrivaled mere speech. The two girls sat staring at the jeweled token before them as though fearing to break the spell their general's message had evoked.

"Isn't it queer?" came from Mary, "I don't feel a bit like crying. When all the nice things happened to me downstairs I wanted to cry. But this letter and my wonderful Shield of Valor make me feel different; as though I'd like to march out and conquer the world!"

Marjorie's red lips curved into a tender smile as she took the pin from the box and fastened it in the folds of lace where Mary's gown fell away at the throat. "That's because it is a true talisman," she reminded softly. "We never knew when long ago we played being soldiers just for fun that we were only getting ready to be soldiers in earnest."

CHAPTER IV—THE NEW SECRETARY

"I'm ready to go to school, Captain!" Marjorie Dean popped her curly head into the living room. "Is the note ready, too? It's simply dear in you to give me a chance to call on Miss Archer."

"Just a moment." Mrs. Dean hastily addressed an envelope and slipped into it the note she had just finished writing. "I could mail it, I suppose, but I thought you might like to play special messenger," she observed, handing Marjorie the note.

"It was a glorious thought," laughed Marjorie. "I wanted to see Miss Archer yesterday, but I didn't like to go to her office on the very first day without a good excuse. Do I look nice, Captain?" she inquired archly.

"You know you do, vain child." Mrs. Dean surveyed the dainty figure of her daughter with pardonable pride. "That quaint flowered organdie frock exactly suits you. Now salute your captain and hurry along. I don't care to have you tardy on my account."

Marjorie embraced her mother in her usual tempestuous fashion and went skipping out of the house and down the stone walk with the joyous abandon of a little girl. Once the gate had swung behind her she dropped into a more decorous gait as she hurried along the wide, shady street toward school. "Oh, goodness!" she murmured. When within two blocks of the high school building she glimpsed the City Hall clock. Its huge, black hands pointed to five minutes to nine. "I'll have to run for it," was her dismayed reflection. "If I hurry, I can make it. I won't have time to put my hat in my new junior locker, though."

Decorum now discarded, Marjorie set off on a brisk run that brought her into the locker room at precisely one minute to nine. Hastily depositing her dainty rose-trimmed leghorn on a convenient window ledge, she ran up the basement stairs to the study hall, gaining the seat assigned to her the previous day just as the nine o'clock bell clanged forth its warning. She smiled rather contemptuously as she noted the disapproving glance Miss Merton flung in her direction. She had escaped a scolding by virtue of a few brief seconds.

"She hasn't changed a bit," was Marjorie's inward judgment, as she turned her gaze upon the rows of students; called together again to continue their earnest march along the road of education. Her heart thrilled with pride as she noted how few vacant seats the great study hall held. The freshman class was unusually large. She noticed there were a number of girls she had never before seen. It looked, too, as though none of last year's freshmen had dropped out of school. As for the juniors, they were all present, even to Mignon La Salle. But how decidedly grown-up the French girl looked! Her black curls were arranged in an ultra-fashionable knot at the back of her head that made her appear several years older than she really was. Her gown, too, an elaborate affair of sage green pongee, with wide bands of heavy insertion, added to her years. She looked very little like a school girl Marjorie thought.

Lost in contemplation of the new Mignon, she was rudely reminded of the fact that she was staring by Mignon herself. Their eyes meeting, Mignon made a face at Marjorie by way of expressing her candid opinion of the girl she disliked. Marjorie colored and hastily looked away, amused rather than angry at this display of childishness. It hardly accorded with her grown-up air. She had not realized that she had been guilty of staring. Her mind was intent on trying to recall something she had heard in connection with the French girl that now eluded her memory. Shrugging her shoulders she dismissed it as a matter of small consequence.

As the members of the four classes were still vacillating between which subjects to take up and which to exclude from their programs of study, classes that morning were to mean a mere business of assembling in the various recitation rooms, there to receive the first instructions from the special teachers before settling down to the usual routine of lessons.

For her junior program, Marjorie had decided upon third year French, English Literature, Cæsar's Commentaries and civil government. As she had recently begun piano lessons, she had wisely concluded that, with piano practice, four subjects would keep her sufficiently busy. Her interest in music had developed as a result of her association with Constance Stevens. She yearned to be able some day to accompany Constance's beautiful voice on the piano. Mrs. Dean had long deplored the fact that Marjorie was not interested in becoming at least a fair pianist. Herself a musician of considerable skill, she believed it a necessary accomplishment for girls and was delighted when Marjorie had announced that she wished to begin lessons on the piano.

By reciting English literature during the first period of the morning and French the second, the last period before noon was hers for study. Civil government and Cæsar recitations the first two periods of the afternoon left her the last hour of that session free. She had always tried to arrange her subjects to gain that coveted afternoon period, and now she felt especially pleased at being able to also reserve the last period of the morning for study.

It was while she sat in her old place in French class, listening to the obsequiously polite adjurations of Professor Fontaine, that she remembered the still undelivered note from her mother to Miss Archer. "I'm a faithless messenger," was her rueful thought. "I'll hurry to Miss Archer's office with Captain's note the minute class is over." Contritely patting a fold of her lace-trimmed blouse where she had tucked the letter for safe-keeping, Marjorie gave strict attention to the earnestly-exhorting instructor.

"Eet ees een thees class that we shall read the great works of the incomparable French awthors," he announced with an impressive roll of r's. "Eet ees of a truth necessary that you should become familiar weeth them. You moost, therefore, stoody your lessons and be thus always preepaired. Eet ees sad when my pupeels come to me with so many fleemsy excuses. Thees year I shall nevaire accept them. I most eenseest that you preepaire each day the lesson for the next."

Marjorie smiled to herself. The long-suffering professor was forever preaching a preparedness, which it never fell to his lot to see diligently practised by the majority of his pupils. Personally, she could not be classed among the guilty. Her love of the musical language kept her interest in it unflagging, thereby making her one of the professor's most dependable props.

The recitation over, she paused to greet the odd little man, who received her with delight, warmly shaking her hand. "Eet ees a grand plaisir thus to see you again, Mees Marjorie," he declared. "Ah, I am assured that you at least weel nevaire say 'oonpreepaired.'"

"I'll try not to. I'm ever so glad to see you, too, Professor Fontaine." After a brief exchange of pleasantries she left the class room a trifle hurriedly and set off to call on Miss Archer.

Entering the spacious living room office, she was forcibly reminded that Marcia Arnold's high school days had ended on the previous June. The pretty room was quite deserted. Marjorie sighed as she glanced toward the vacant chair, drawn under the closed desk that had been Marcia's. How much she would miss her old friend. Since that day long past on which they had come to an understanding, she and Marcia had found much in common. Marjorie sighed regretfully, wondering who Miss Archer's next secretary would be.

As there was no one about to announce her, she walked slowly toward the half-closed door of the inner office. Pausing just outside, she peeped in. Her eyes widened with surprise as she caught sight of an unfamiliar figure. A tall, very attractive young woman stood before the principal's desk, busily engaged in the perusal of a printed sheet of paper which she held in her hand. It looked as though Miss Archer had already secured someone in Marcia's place.

"May I come in, please?" Marjorie asked sweetly, halting in the doorway.

The girl at the desk uttered a faint exclamation. The paper she held fluttered to the desk. A wave of color dyed her exquisitely tinted skin as she turned a pair of large, startled, black eyes upon the intruder. For a second the two girls eyed each other steadily. Marjorie conceived a curious impression that she had seen this stranger before, yet it was too vague to convey to her the slightest knowledge of the other's identity.

"You are Miss Archer's new secretary, are you not?" she asked frankly. "You can tell me, perhaps, where to find her. I have a note to deliver to her personally."

A quick shade of relief crossed the other girl's suddenly flushing face. Smiling in self-possessed fashion, she said, "Miss Archer will not be back directly. I cannot tell you when she will return."

"I think I'll wait here for her," decided Marjorie. "I have no recitation this period."

The stranger's arched brows arched themselves a trifle higher. "As you please," she returned indifferently. She again turned her attention to the papers on the desk.

Seating herself on the wide oak bench, Marjorie took speculative stock of the new secretary. "What a stunning girl," was her mental opinion. "She's dressed rather too well for a secretary, though," flashed across her as she noted the smart gown of white china silk, the very cut of which pointed to the work of a high-priced modiste. "I suppose she's getting examination papers ready for the new pupils. I wonder why she doesn't sit down."

As she thus continued to cogitate regarding the stranger, the girl frowned deeply at another paper she had picked up and swung suddenly about. "Are you just entering high school?" she asked with direct abruptness.

"Oh, no." Marjorie smilingly shook her head. "I am a junior."

"Are you?" The stranger again lost herself in puzzled contemplation of the paper. Hearing an approaching footfall she made a quick move toward the center of the office, raising her eyes sharply to greet a girl who had come in quest of Miss Archer. Promptly disposing of the seeker, she returned to her task. Several times after that she was interrupted by the entrance of various students, whom she received coolly and dismissed with, "Not here. I don't know when Miss Archer will return." Marjorie noted idly that with every fresh arrival, the young woman continued to move well away from the desk.

Marjorie watched her in fascination. She was undoubtedly beautiful in a strangely bold fashion, but apparently very cold and self-centered. She had received the students who had entered the office with a brusqueness that bordered on discourtesy. Two or three of them, whom Marjorie knew, had greeted her in friendly fashion, at the same time mutely questioning with uplifted brows as to whom this stranger might be.

"This problem in quadratic equations is a terror," the girl at the desk suddenly remarked, her finger pointing to a row of algebraic symbols on the paper she was still clutching. "Algebra's awfully hard, isn't it?"

"I always liked it," returned Marjorie, glad of a chance to break the silence. "What is the problem?"

"Come here," ordered the other girl. "I don't call that an easy problem. Do you?"

Marjorie rose and approached the desk. The stranger handed her the paper, indexing the vexatious problem.

"Oh, that's not so very hard," was Marjorie's light response.

"Can you work it out?" came the short inquiry, a note of suppressed eagerness in the questioner's voice.

"Why, I suppose so. Can't you?"

"I was trying it before you came in just for fun. I've forgotten my algebra, I guess. I don't believe I got the right result. It's rather good practice to review, isn't it?"

"She must be a senior," sprang to Marjorie's mind. Aloud, she agreed that it was. "I ought not to have forgotten my algebra," she added. "It's only a year since I finished it."

"See if you think I did this right, will you? I'm curious to know." The stranger thrust into her hand a second paper, covered with figures.

Marjorie inspected it, feeling only mildly interested. "No; you made a mistake here. It goes this way. Have you a pencil?"

The pencil promptly forthcoming, the obliging junior seated herself at a nearby table and diligently went to work. So busy was she that she failed to note the covert glances which her companion sent now and then toward the door. But, during the brief space of time in which Marjorie was engaged with the difficult equation, no one came. Altogether she had not been in the office longer than fifteen minutes. To her it seemed at least half an hour.

"Here you are." She tendered the finished work to the other girl, who seized it eagerly with a brief, "Thank you. I can see where I made my mistake when I have time to compare the two." With a smile, which Marjorie thought a trifle patronizing, she carelessly nodded her gratitude. Laying the printed examination sheet on a pile of similar papers, she placed a weight upon them and walked gracefully from the office, taking with her the two sheets of paper, bearing the results of her own and Marjorie's labor.

Another fifteen minutes went by. Still no one came, except a student or two in quest of Miss Archer. Marjorie decided that she would wait no longer. She would come back again that afternoon, before the second session opened. It was almost noon. Were she to return to the study hall just then, it meant to court the caustic rebuke of Miss Merton. The locker room offered her a temporary refuge. Accordingly, she wended her steps toward it.

"Where were you that last period?" demanded Jerry Macy, coming up behind her as she stood at the mirror adjusting her rose-weighted hat.

"Oh, Jerry! How you startled me." Marjorie swung about. "I was up in Miss Archer's office."

"So soon?" teased Jerry, putting on a shocked expression. "I am surprised."

"Don't be so suspicious," responded Marjorie, adopting Jerry's bantering tone. "I had a note, if you please, from Captain, to deliver to Miss Archer. I saw the new secretary, too."

"Humph!" ejaculated Jerry. "You must have only thought you saw her. So far as I know Miss Archer hasn't secured a secretary yet."

"But she must have," Marjorie insisted. "There was a tall girl in her office when I went there. She must surely be the girl to take Marcia's place, for she was standing at Miss Archer's desk, going over some papers."

"That's funny. What did she look like? You said she was tall?"

"Yes; tall and very pretty. She had big, black eyes and perfectly gorgeous auburn hair——" Marjorie broke off with a puzzled frown. Her own words had a curious reminiscent ring. Someone else had said the very same thing about——Who had said it, and about whom had it been said?

"Now I know you didn't see Miss Archer's new secretary," cried Jerry in triumph. "There's only one person that can answer to your description. She's that Rowena Farnham I told you about, Mignon's side partner. I told you she was going to enter the sophomore class. She was probably waiting for Miss Archer herself. She has to try her exams, I suppose."

"But what was she doing at Miss Archer's desk?" asked Marjorie sharply. "Why did she answer me and make me think she was the secretary? She told several other girls that Miss Archer was out!"

"Search me," replied Jerry inelegantly. "If she's much like Mignon it's hard to tell what she was up to. Believe me, they're a precious pair of trouble-makers and don't you forget it."

"I ought to have recognized her," faltered Marjorie. A curious sense of dread had stolen over her. "Don't you remember Mary described her almost as I did just now, that day you came to see us, when first you got back to Sanford?"

"Well, nobody's going to kill you because you didn't, are they?" inquired Jerry with a grin. "What's the matter? What makes you look so solemn?"

"Oh, I was just wondering," evaded Marjorie. Outwardly only slightly ruffled, tumult raged within. She had begun to see clearly what had hitherto been obscure and the revelation was a severe shock. All she could hope was that what she now strongly suspected might not, after all, be true.

CHAPTER V—A STORMY INTERVIEW

Marjorie returned to school that afternoon in a most perturbed state of mind, occasioned by Jerry Macy's identification of Rowena Farnham as the girl whom she had assisted in the working out of the problem in quadratic equations. She was now almost certain that she had unwittingly assisted in a most dishonest enterprise. If the papers on Miss Archer's desk comprised the trial examination to sophomore estate, then Rowena had no doubt been guilty of tampering with what should concern her only at the moment when the test began. If they were the sophomore examination papers, why had Miss Archer left them thus exposed on her desk? And now what was she, Marjorie, to do about it? She felt that when she delivered her mother's note to Miss Archer, she ought to inform the principal of what had occurred during her absence. Yet she hated to do this. It was tale bearing. Besides, her suspicions might prove unfounded.

She was still juggling the trying situation when she entered Miss Archer's office to deliver her captain's note. Should she speak of it or not? The fact that Miss Archer was now accessible but extremely busy, with several girls occupying the office benches, caused her to put off her decision for a time. She stopped only long enough to receive a kindly welcome from the principal and to perform her mission as messenger. Then she went dejectedly to her recitation in civil government, wondering resentfully if the event of the morning was the beginning of an unpleasant year.

By a determined effort of will, Marjorie put the whole thing aside to attend strictly to her recitations. But during the study hour that preceded dismissal for the day, a way of settling the difficulty presented itself to her. It was not an agreeable way, but her straightforward soul welcomed it as a means toward settlement. She was resolved to seek Rowena Farnham and learn the truth. The question of where to find her was next to be considered. She had not yet made an appearance into the study hall. Doubtless she was in the little recitation room on the second floor that was seldom used except in the case of pupils with special examinations to try. Marjorie mused darkly as to whether the problem she had obligingly solved would figure in Rowena's algebra paper.

Half-past three saw Marjorie on her way to the locker room, keeping a sharp lookout for a tall figure crowned with luxuriant auburn hair. Her vigilance met with no reward, however, and she left the school building in company with Irma, Jerry, Constance and Susan, deliberating as to what she had best do next. Outside the high school she caught no glimpse of her quarry among the throng of girls that came trooping down the wide stone steps.

Although she took part in her friends' animated conversation, she was steadily thinking of the self-imposed task that lay before her.

"Let's go down to Sargent's," proposed Susan, gleefully jingling a handful of silver that clinked of sundaes and divers delicious cheer.

"You girls go. I can't. I've an errand to do." Marjorie's color rose as she spoke.

"Do your errand some other time," coaxed Susan. "I may not have any money to spend to-morrow."

"I'll treat to-morrow," Marjorie assured her. "I can't possibly put off my errand. You can imagine I'm with you. Always cultivate your imagination."

Four voices rose to protest her decision, but she remained firm. "To-morrow," she compromised. "Please don't tease me. I can't really go with you to-day."

"We'll try to get along without you, just this once," agreed tactful Constance. Something in Marjorie's manner told her that her friend wished to go on her way alone.

"Go ahead then, Marjorie. Do your errand, faithful child," consented Jerry, who had also scented the unusual and shrewdly speculated as to whether it had anything to do with their conversation of the morning.

Anxious, yet regretful, to be free of her chums, Marjorie said good-bye and hurried off in an opposite direction. Jerry had said that the Farnhams lived in the beautiful residence that adjoined Mignon La Salle's home. It was not a long walk, yet how Marjorie dreaded it. Given that Rowena were at home, Mignon would, perhaps, be with her. That would make matters doubly hard. Yet she could do no less than carry out the interview she felt must take place at the earliest possible moment.

It was a very grave little girl who opened the ornamental iron gate and proceeded reluctantly up the long driveway to the huge brown stone house, set in the midst of a wide expanse of tree-dotted lawn. For all the residence was a magnificent affair, Marjorie shivered as she mounted the massive stone steps. There was little of the atmosphere of home about it.

"Is Miss Rowena Farnham here?" was her low-voiced question of the white-capped maid who answered the door.

"She hasn't come home from school yet, miss," informed the maid. "Will you step into the house and wait for her?"

"Yes, thank you." Marjorie followed the woman into a high-ceilinged, beautifully appointed, square hall and across it to a mammoth drawing-room, very handsomely furnished, but cheerless, nevertheless. She felt very small and insignificant as she settled herself lightly on an ornate gilt chair, to await the arrival of Rowena.

Her vigil was destined to be tedious, unbroken by the sight of anyone save the maid, who passed through the hall once or twice on her way to answer the bell. Even she did not trouble herself to glance through the half-parted brocade portieres at the lonely little figure in the room beyond. Consulting her wrist watch, Marjorie read five o'clock. She had been waiting for over an hour. She guessed that the girl on whom she had come to call must be with Mignon La Salle. There was at least a grain of comfort for her in this conjecture. If Mignon were at home now, there was small chance that she would be present at the interview.

An impatient hand on the bell sent a shrill, reverberating peal through the great house. An instant and she heard the maid's voice, carefully lowered. There came the sound of quick, questioning tones, which she recognized. Rowena had at last put in an appearance. Immediately there followed a flinging back of the concealing portieres and the girl who had sprung into Marjorie's knowledge so unbecomingly that morning walked into the room.

"You wished to see——Oh, it's you!" The tall girl's black eyes swept her uninvited guest with an expression far from cordial.

"Yes, it is I," Marjorie's inflection was faintly satirical. "I made a mistake about you this morning. I thought you were Miss Archer's new secretary." She lost no time in going directly to the point.

For answer Rowena threw back her auburn head and laughed loudly. "I fooled you nicely, didn't I?" According to outward signs her conscience was apparently untroubled.

"Yes," returned Marjorie quietly. "Why did you do it?"

Rowena's laughing lips instantly took on a belligerent curve. The very evenness of the inquiry warned her that trouble was brewing for her. "See here," she began rudely, "what did you come to my house for? I'm not pleased to see you. Judging from several things I've heard, I don't care to know you."

Marjorie paled at the rebuff. She had half expected it, yet now that it had come she did not relish it. At first meeting she had been irritated by the other girl's almost rude indifference. Now she had dropped all semblance of courtesy.

"I hardly think it matters about your knowing or not knowing me," she retorted in the same carefully schooled tone. "You, of course, are the one to decide that. What does matter is this—I must ask you to tell me exactly why you wished me to work out that quadratic problem for you. It is quite necessary that I should know."

"Why is it so necessary?"

"Because I must believe one of two things," was Marjorie's grave response. "I must have the truth. I won't be kept in the dark about it. Either you only pretended to play secretary as a rather peculiar joke, or else you did it purposely because——" She hesitated, half ashamed to accuse the other of dishonesty.

"What will you do if I say I did it on purpose?" tantalized Rowena. "Go to your Miss Archer, I suppose, with a great tale about me. I understand that is one of your little pastimes. Now listen to me, and remember what I say. You think I was prying into those examination papers, don't you?"

"I'd rather not think so." Marjorie raised an honest, appealing glance to meet the mocking gleam of Rowena's black eyes.

"Who cares what you think? You are a goody-goody, and I never saw one yet that I'd walk across the street with. Whatever I want, I always get. Remember that, too. If your dear Miss Archer hadn't been called to another part of the building, I might never have had a chance to read over those examinations. She went away in a hurry and left me sitting in the office. Naturally, as her desk was open, I took a look to see what there was to see. I wasn't afraid of any subject but algebra. I'm n. g. in that. So I was pretty lucky to get a chance to read over the examination. I knew right away by the questions that it was the one I'd have to try.

"My father promised me a pearl necklace if I'd pass all my tests for the sophomore class. Of course I wanted to win it. That quadratic problem counted thirty credits. It meant that without it I'd stand no chance to pass algebra. I couldn't do it, and I was in despair when you came into the office. If you hadn't been so stupid as to take me for Miss Archer's secretary and hadn't said you were a junior, I'd have let you alone. That secretary idea wasn't bad, though. It sent those other girls about their business. I thought you could do that problem if I couldn't. It's a good thing you did. I copied it in examination this afternoon and I know it's right," she ended triumphantly.

Sheer amazement of the girl's bold confession rendered Marjorie silent. Never in all her life had she met a girl like Rowena Farnham. Her calm admittance to what Marjorie had suspected was unbelievable. And she appeared to feel no shame for her dishonesty. She gloried in it. Finding her voice at last, the astounded and dismayed interviewer said with brave firmness: "I can't look at this so lightly, Miss Farnham. It wasn't fair in you to deceive me into doing a thing like that."

"What's done can't be undone," quoted Rowena, seemingly undisturbed by the reproof. "You are as deep in the mud as I am in the mire. You helped me, you know."

"I will not be included in such dishonesty." Marjorie sprang angrily to her feet and faced Rowena. "If Miss Archer knew this she would not accept your algebra paper. She might not wish to accept you as a pupil, either. I hoped when I came here this afternoon that everything would turn out all right, after all. I hoped that paper might not be the algebra test you were to have. I don't wish to tell Miss Archer, yet it's not fair to either of us that you should masquerade under false colors. You have put me in a very hard position."

It was now Rowena who grew angry. During the interview she had remained standing, looking down on the girl in the chair with amused contempt. Marjorie's flash of resentment unleashed a temper that had ever been the despair of Rowena's father and mother. Her dark eyes glowed like live coals, her tall, slender body shook with fury. "If you dare go to Miss Archer with what I've told you, I'll put you in a much harder position. I'll make you lose every friend you have in school. I know all about you. You've bullied and snubbed poor Mignon La Salle and made her lose her friends. But you can't bully or threaten or snub me. I didn't want to come to Sanford to live. It's nothing but a little, silly country town. I didn't want to go to your old school. My father and mother make me go. My father doesn't believe in select boarding schools, so I have to make the best of it. If I pass my examinations into the sophomore class I'll make it my business to see that I get whatever I take a notion to have. You can't stop me. I've always done as I pleased at home and I'll do as I please in school. If you tell Miss Archer about this morning, I'll see that you get more blame than I. Don't forget that, either."

Marjorie felt as though she had been caught in a pelting rain of hail-stones. Yet the furious flow of vituperation which beat down upon her did not in the least intimidate her. "I am not afraid of anything you may do or say," she returned, a staunch little figure of dignified scorn. "I came to see you in all good faith, willing to give you the benefit of the doubt. Now that I understand exactly how you feel about this affair, I won't trouble you further. Good afternoon."

"Stop! What are you going to do?" called Rowena. Marjorie had already passed into the hall. "You've got to tell me before you leave this house." She darted after her steadily retreating caller, cheeks flaming.

At the outer door, Marjorie paused briefly, her hand on the dead latch. "I said 'good afternoon,'" was her sole response. Then she let herself out and walked proudly away from the house of inhospitality, oblivious to the torrent of hot words which the irate Rowena shrieked after her from the veranda.

CHAPTER VI—A QUESTION OF SCHOOL-GIRL HONOR

"I've something to report, Captain." Marjorie entered her mother's room and dropped dispiritedly at her feet. Unpinning her flower-decked hat, she removed it with a jerk and let it slide to the floor.

"Well, dear, what is it?" Mrs. Dean cast a half anxious look at her daughter. The long strip of pink crochet work, destined to become part of an afghan for Marjorie's "house" dropped from her hands. Reaching down she gave the dejected curly head at her knee a reassuring pat. "What has happened to spoil my little girl's second day at school?"

Marjorie flashed an upward glance at her mother that spoke volumes. "I've had a horrid time to-day," she answered. "Last year, when things didn't go right, I kept some of them to myself. This year I'm going to tell you everything." Her voice quivering with indignation at the calamity that had overtaken her unawares, she related the disturbing events that had so recently transpired. "I don't know what to do," she ended. "Do you think I ought to go to Miss Archer and tell her everything?"

"That is a leading question, Lieutenant." Mrs. Dean continued a sympathetic smoothing of Marjorie's curls. "It is one thing to confess one's own faults; it is quite another to make public the faults of someone else. It is hardly fair to Miss Archer to allow this girl to profit by her own dishonesty. It is not fair to the girl herself. If she is allowed to pursue, unchecked, a course which will eventually lead to a great dishonesty, then you would be in a measure responsible. On the other hand, I abhor a talebearer. I can't decide at once what you ought to do. I shall have to think it over and give you my answer later. Your rights must be considered also. You were an innocent party to a despicable act, therefore I do not believe that you owe the author of it any special loyalty. I am not sure but that I ought to go to Miss Archer myself about it. You have suffered a good deal, since you began going to Sanford High School, through Mignon La Salle. I do not propose that this new girl shall spoil your junior year for you. Come to me to-morrow at this time and I will have made up my mind what is best for you. I am glad you told me this."

"So am I," sighed Marjorie. "I know that whatever you decide will be best for me, Captain. I am not afraid for myself. It's only that I hate to make trouble for this girl, even though she deserves it. You see it may mean a good deal to her father and mother to have her get along well in school. She said her father wouldn't let her go away to boarding school. That sounds as though he wanted her to be at home where he could look after her."

"That must also be considered," agreed Mrs. Dean. "Now don't worry about this affair any more. I am sure we shall find the wisest way out of it for everyone concerned. You had better run along now and get ready for dinner. It's almost half-past six."

Marjorie reached for her discarded hat. Scrambling to her feet she embraced her mother and went to her room, infinitely cheered. As she left the room, Mrs. Dean sent after her a glance freighted with motherly protection. She had no sympathy for a girl such as Marjorie had described Rowena Farnham to be, and she uttered a mental prayer of thankfulness that her own daughter was above reproach.

No further mention of the affair was made between mother and daughter that evening. Nevertheless, Marjorie went to school the next morning in a far from buoyant mood. She had been wakened by a reverberating roll of thunder, followed by the furious beating of rain against her windows. A true child of sunshine, the steady tapping of the heavy drops filled her with a dread sense of oppression which she could not shake off.

By noon, however, it had passed away with the storm. When she went home to luncheon the sun was high in the sky. The rain-washed streets were rapidly succumbing to his warm smile. Only a puddle here and there, or a shower of silver drops from a breeze-shaken tree remained to remind her of the morning deluge.

Returning from luncheon, she had hardly gained her seat when Miss Merton stalked down the aisle to her desk. "Report to Miss Archer at once, Miss Dean," she commanded in her most disagreeable manner.

Marjorie's thoughts immediately flew to yesterday. Was it possible that Rowena Farnham had gone to the principal of her own volition? It was hardly to be credited. Remembering her mother's note, Marjorie jumped to the conclusion that this was the most probable reason for the summons.

"Good afternoon, Marjorie," greeted Miss Archer from her desk, as the pretty junior appeared in the doorway. "Come here, my dear. I have something rather unusual to show you." She motioned Marjorie to draw up a chair beside her own. "I wonder if you can throw any light upon this."

"This" was an open letter, which she now tendered to the puzzled girl. Marjorie read:

"Miss Archer:

"Yesterday morning, at a little after eleven o'clock, Marjorie Dean and a girl with red hair and black eyes, whose name I do not know, meddled with the examination papers on your desk while you were in another part of the building. Marjorie Dean showed the girl how to do one of the examination problems in algebra. This I know because I heard them talking about it and saw them have the list of questions. Such dishonesty is a disgrace to Sanford High School.

"The Observer."

Marjorie allowed the letter to fall from her nerveless hands. She felt herself grow hot and cold as she forced herself to meet Miss Archer's intent scrutiny. Yet she said nothing. Only her brown eyes sent forth agonized signals of distress.

Noting her strange demeanor, Miss Archer's pleasant face hardened. Was Marjorie Dean really guilty of such dishonor? If innocent, why did she not hotly proclaim the fact? "I am waiting for you to explain the meaning of this note, Marjorie," she reminded sternly. "Can you do so?"

"Yes," came the low monosyllable.

"Then do so at once," crisply ordered the principal.

Marjorie drew a long breath. "I can't explain my part of it without bringing in someone else," she faltered.

"You mean Miss Farnham, I suppose?"

Marjorie hesitated, then nodded. It appeared that Miss Archer had already put two and two together.

"I happen to know that Miss Farnham is the only one who could possibly answer to the description this letter gives," continued Miss Archer impatiently. "She was also the only one to be interested in the papers on my desk. I sent for you first, however, because I wished to give you a chance to explain how you happened to figure in this affair. I have always had a great deal of faith in you, Marjorie. I do not wish to lose that faith. Now I must insist on knowing exactly what occurred here yesterday morning. Did you or did you not assist Miss Farnham in solving a problem in algebra, which she culled from the examination paper in that subject?"

"Miss Archer," Marjorie said earnestly, "I did help Miss Farnham with that problem, but I had no idea that she was trying to do anything so dishonorable. It all came about through a mistake. I'd rather she would explain that part of it. The reason I happened to be in this office was because of the note my mother asked me to bring you. Miss Farnham was here when I came in. While I sat waiting for you she asked me to help her with that problem. I solved it for her and she took it and went away. I waited a little longer, then left the office."

Miss Archer's stern features gradually relaxed as Marjorie made this straightforward account of her own actions. The principal noted, however, that she had revealed considerably less regarding the other girl. "That is a somewhat indefinite statement," she said slowly. "You have not been frank as to Miss Farnham. You are keeping something back. You must tell me all. I prefer to know the absolute facts from you before sending for the other party to this affair."

"Please don't ask me to tell you, Miss Archer," pleaded Marjorie. "I'd rather not."

Miss Archer frowned, This was not the first time that Marjorie had taken such a stubborn stand. She knew the young girl's horror of telling tales. Yet here was something that she deemed it necessary to uncover. She did not relish being thus balked by a too rigid standard of school-girl honor. It suddenly occurred to her to wonder how Marjorie could have been so easily deceived.

"Do you think this is fair to me?" she questioned sharply. "I feel that I have behaved very fairly to you in thus far assuming that you are innocent. There are gaps in your story which must be filled. I wish you, not Miss Farnham, to supply them. Suppose I were to say, it is very strange that you did not suspect this girl of trickery."

"But I didn't, truly I didn't," sounded the half-tearful protest.

"I am not actually saying that you suspected her. Tell me this, at least. Did you know that the problem she asked you to solve for her was from the examination sheet?"

"I—she——" stammered the unfortunate junior.

"You did know it, then!" exclaimed Miss Archer in pained suspicion. "This places you in a bad light. If you knew the source of the problem you can hardly claim innocence now unless you give me absolute proof of it."

"You have my word that I am not guilty." Her desire to cry vanished. Marjorie now spoke with gentle dignity. "I try always to be truthful."

Miss Archer surveyed the unobliging witness in vexed silence. At heart she believed Marjorie to be innocent, but she was rapidly losing patience. "Since you won't be frank with me, I shall interview Miss Farnham as soon as she finishes her examinations of the morning. I shall not allow her to go on with this afternoon's test until I have reached the bottom of this affair. Come to my office as soon as you return from luncheon. That is all." The principal made a dignified gesture of dismissal.

The beseeching glance poor Marjorie directed toward Miss Archer was lost upon the now incensed woman. She had already begun to busy herself at her desk. If she had glimpsed the reproach of those mournful eyes, it is doubtful whether she would have been impressed by them. Secretly she was wondering whether she had made the mistake of reposing too much confidence in Marjorie Dean.

CHAPTER VII—FAITH AND UNFAITH

On reaching home that noon Marjorie's first impulse was to hurry to her mother with a recital of the morning's events. Greatly to her dismay, Delia met her at the door with the announcement that her mistress had motored to a neighboring town to meet Mr. Dean, who had telegraphed her from there. They would not arrive home in time for luncheon, probably not until late in the afternoon.

Divided between the pleasure of seeing her father and distress occasioned by Miss Archer's implied disbelief, Marjorie ate a lonely and most unsatisfactory luncheon. She could think of nothing other than the impending session in which she and Rowena Farnham would so soon figure. She pondered gloomily on the strange way in which the knowledge of Rowena's unscrupulous behavior had been borne to Miss Archer. Who could have written that letter? Could it be laid at the door of one of the several girls who had inquired for the principal and promptly retired from the scene? If this were so, then some one of them must have lingered just outside to spy upon herself and Rowena. She knew the majority of those who had sought the office while she lingered there. Only one or two had been strangers. Of those she knew, she could recall no one of them she would deem guilty of spying.

As she left her home for the high school, Marjorie smiled in wry fashion at the thought of Rowena's anger when she learned that her unfair tactics had been discovered and reported. If she treated Miss Archer to a scene similar to that which Marjorie had undergone in Rowena's home, she was very likely to find herself out of high school before having actually entered. As it was, Rowena stood a strong chance of forfeiting the privilege to try the remainder of her examinations.

Twenty minutes past one found Marjorie on the threshold of the principal's office. At sight of her Miss Archer bowed distantly and went on with her writing. As yet Rowena had not put in an appearance. Ten minutes later she strolled nonchalantly in, her bold, black eyes registering supreme contempt of the world in general. Her smart gown of delft blue crêpe set off her dazzlingly fair skin and heavy auburn hair to perfection. She was a stunning young person, and well aware of her good looks.

"I understand you wish to see me," she drawled in a tone bordering on impatience. Ignoring Marjorie, save for one swift, menacing glance, she addressed herself to the woman at the desk.

Miss Archer had already risen. Now she fixed the newcomer with stern, searching eyes. "Sit over there, Miss Farnham." She waved her to a seat beside Marjorie on the oak bench.

With an insolent shrugging of her shoulders, Rowena sat down, placing the length of the bench between herself and its other occupant. "Well, what is it?" she asked unconcernedly.

Miss Archer's lips compressed themselves a trifle more firmly. "Your manner is distinctly disrespectful, Miss Farnham. Kindly remember to whom you are speaking."

Rowena's shoulders again went into eloquent play. "Oh, excuse me," she murmured.

Ignoring the discourtesy, Miss Archer reached to her desk for the letter, the contents of which Marjorie already knew. Handing it to Rowena she said: "Read this letter. You will then understand why I sent for you."

Looking distinctly bored, the girl perused the letter. A tantalizing smile curved her red lips as she finished. "This is your work," she accused, turning to Marjorie.

The latter opened her brown eyes in genuine amazement. The accusation was totally unexpected. "You know very well it is not," she flung back, the pink in her cheeks deepening.

"Whatever you have to say, Miss Farnham, you may say to me," reproved the principal. "I have already gone over the contents of this letter with Miss Dean."

"I have nothing to say," replied Rowena serenely.

"But I have several things to say to you," reminded Miss Archer sharply. "I demand a complete explanation of what occurred here during my absence yesterday morning."

"I am afraid you've come to the wrong person, then." Rowena was coolly defiant. "Miss Dean can answer your question better than I. No doubt she has already said a number of pleasant things about me."

"Miss Dean has said nothing to your discredit. In fact she has refused to commit herself. She prefers that you do the explaining." Unconsciously Miss Archer sprang into irritated defense of Marjorie.

Rowena's black eyebrows lifted themselves. So the goody-goody had refused to betray her! This was decidedly interesting. Her clever brain at once leaped to the conclusion that with Marjorie's lips sealed it would be hard to establish her own dishonesty. In itself the letter offered no actual proof. It was merely signed "The Observer." A cunning expression crept into her eyes. "Someone must have been trying to play a joke," she now airily suggested. "The very fact that the letter isn't properly signed goes to prove that."

"Miss Farnham!" The principal's authoritative utterance betrayed her great displeasure. "You are overstepping all bounds. Miss Dean herself has admitted that she solved an algebraic problem for you. I insist on knowing whether or not that problem was taken from an examination sheet that lay among others on my desk. If so, there is but one inference to be drawn. During my absence you tampered with the papers on my desk. No such thing has ever before occurred in the history of this school. Now I ask you pointblank, did you or did you not meddle with my papers?"

Without replying, Rowena's eyes roved shrewdly to Marjorie, as though trying to discover what the latter intended to do. Were she to reply to the question in the negative, would this baby of a girl, whom she already despised, still maintain silence?

Apparently, Marjorie read her thought. "Miss Farnham," she broke in, her soft voice ringing with purpose, "if you do not answer Miss Archer truthfully, I, at least, will."

That settled it. Nevertheless, Rowena determined that Marjorie should pay for her interference. "If you must know," she said sullenly, "I did glance over them. You had no business to leave them on the desk. Miss Dean saw me do it, too, but she didn't seem to mind. I even showed her that problem in quadratics and told her I couldn't do it. So she did it for me."

"Is this true?" To the distressed listener Miss Archer's amazed question came as a faint and far-off sound. Driven into a corner by Rowena's spiteful misrepresentation, Marjorie determined to clear herself of the opprobrium. "I saw Miss Farnham with the papers," she affirmed. "She pointed out to me the one she couldn't do and I solved it for her. I thought——"

"That will do." Never to Marjorie's recollection had Miss Archer's voice carried with it such unmeasured severity. For once she was too thoroughly displeased to be just. Only that morning Marjorie had earnestly proclaimed her innocence. Brought face to face with Rowena, she had renigged, or so it now seemed to the affronted principal. Abhoring deceit and untruthfulness, she rashly ticketed her hitherto favorite pupil with both faults.

"But Miss Archer," pleaded Marjorie desperately, "won't you allow me to——"

"It strikes me that too much has already been said that might better have been left unsaid," cut in the principal coldly. "You two young women are guilty of a most despicable bit of work. If it lay within my power I would expel both of you from the school you have disgraced. This matter will be taken up by the Board of Education. All I can do is to send you both home, there to await the decision of those above me. Your parents shall be informed at once of what has taken place. As for you, Miss Farnham, in case the Board decides to give you another chance you will be obliged to take an entirely new set of examinations. In a measure I hold myself responsible for this. I should have locked my desk. I have always trusted my pupils. Dishonesty on the part of two of them is a severe blow. You may both leave the school at once. You, Miss Dean, need not return to the study hall."

Rowena Farnham received her dismissal with an elaborate shrug that plainly indicated how little she cared. Without deigning a reply she strolled out of the office, apparently as self-possessed as when she had entered. Marjorie, however, remained rooted to the bench on which she sat. She could not believe the evidence of her own ears. Neither could she credit the principal's sudden unjust stand.

"Miss Archer," she faltered, "won't you——"

"The subject is closed, Miss Dean. Kindly leave my office." Miss Archer refused to meet the two pleading eyes that persistently sought hers. This self-revelation of the girl's guilt had dealt her a hurt which she could not soon forget. To uncover treachery and dishonesty in a friend is an experience which carries with it its own bitterness. The very fact that it is unexpected makes it infinitely harder to bear. Miss Archer's disappointment in Marjorie was so great as to obscure her usually clear insight into matters. She had trusted her so implicitly. She felt as though she could not endure her presence in the office. Now she kept her gaze resolutely fixed on her desk, nor did she alter it until the echo of the misjudged lieutenant's light footfalls had entirely died away.

CHAPTER VIII—FOR THE GOOD OF THE ARMY

Marjorie could never quite recall the details of that dreadful walk home. Only once before in her short life had she been so utterly crushed. That was on the day she had rushed from the little gray house, believing that her beloved Constance was a thief. Now it came back to her with force. Just as she had felt on that terrible afternoon, so must Miss Archer be feeling now. Miss Archer thought that she, Marjorie Dean, was unworthy to be a pupil of Sanford High. "If only Miss Archer had listened to me," surged through her troubled brain as she walked the seemingly endless road home. What would Captain and General say?

Yet with this thought a gleam of daylight pierced the dark. Her Captain already knew all. She knew her daughter to be innocent of wrongdoing. General would believe in her, too. They would not see her thus disgraced without a hearing. She would yet be able to prove to Miss Archer that she was blameless of such dishonesty.

"Well, well!" She had mounted the steps of her home when a cheery voice thus called out to her. The next instant she was in her father's arms. Delight in seeing him, coupled with all she had just undergone, broke down the difficult composure she had managed to maintain while in Miss Archer's presence. With a little sob, Marjorie threw herself into her father's arms, pillowing her curly head against his comforting shoulder.

"My dear child, what has happened?" Mrs. Dean regarded her daughter's shaking shoulders with patient anxiety as she cried out the startled question.

"There, there, Lieutenant." Mr. Dean gathered the weeping girl close in his protecting arms. "Surely you aren't crying because your worthy general has come home?"

"No-o-o," came the muffled protest. "I'm—glad. It's—not—that. I've—been—suspended—from—school."

"What!" Mr. Dean raised the weeper's head from his shoulders and gazed deep into the overflowing brown eyes.

"It's true," gulped Marjorie. "I'm not—to—blame—though. It's all—a—misunderstanding."

"Then we'll straighten it out," soothed Mr. Dean. "Come, now. You and Captain and I will go into the living room and sit right down on the nice comfy davenport. Then you can wail your troubles into our sympathetic ears. Your superior officers will stand by you. You take one arm, Captain, and I'll take the other."

Resigning herself to the guidance of those who loved her best, Marjorie suffered herself to be led into the living room and deposited on the friendly davenport, a solicitous parent on either side.

"You're wonderful, both of you," she sighed, possessing herself of a hand of each. Her brief gust of grief had spent itself. Her voice was now almost steady.

Mrs. Dean had already made a shrewd guess regarding the reason for Marjorie's tears. "Is that affair of yesterday responsible for your suspension from school, Lieutenant?" she questioned abruptly.

"Yes." With an occasional quaver in her speech, Marjorie went over the details of both visits to the principal's office.

"Hm!" ejaculated Mr. Dean, his eyes seeking his wife's. "Suppose you tell your general the beginning of all this."

"It strikes me that Miss Archer behaved in a rather high-handed manner," he observed dryly when Marjorie had ended her sad little story.

"I can't blame her so much." Marjorie was loyal to the death. "I know just how terribly it must have hurt her. I suppose I should have told her everything in the first place."

Mrs. Dean released Marjorie's hand and rose from the davenport, intense determination written on every feature. "Miss Archer will listen to me," she announced grimly. "I shall go to Sanford High School at once. My daughter is entitled to justice and she shall receive it. I am surprised at Miss Archer's unfair attitude. Go upstairs and bathe your face, Marjorie. General, will you see to the car?"

"But she won't see me, I am afraid."

"Nonsense," returned her mother with unusual brusqueness. Stepping into the hall, she consulted the telephone directory. "Give me Sycamore ," she called into the transmitter. "Miss Archer? This is Mrs. Dean. Marjorie has just come from school. I am sure you will accept my word that she has done nothing dishonest. Will it be convenient for you to see us at once? Thank you. We will be at the high school within the next half hour."

During the short telephone conversation, Marjorie stood at her mother's side, hardly daring to breathe. Mrs. Dean hung up the receiver to the accompaniment of her daughter's wild embrace. "Go and make yourself presentable," she chided. Disengaging the clinging arms, she gave Marjorie a gentle shove toward the stairs.

Youth's tears are quickly dried, its sorrows soon forgotten. Ten minutes afterward, a radiant-faced lieutenant presented herself in the hall, renewed buoyancy in her step as she and her captain passed through the gate to where the automobile awaited them with Mr. Dean at the wheel.

"I'll stay here," he decided as they drew up before the high school. "Let our valiant captain lead the charge. You can fall back on your reserves if you are routed with slaughter."

"Captain's won half the battle," joyfully declared Marjorie. "Now I am sure I can win the other half." Blowing a kiss to her father she set her face toward vindication.

Miss Archer greeted Mrs. Dean in a friendly, impersonal fashion, which showed plainly that she was not displeased with the latter for taking such prompt action. Her bow to Marjorie was distinctly reserved, however. She had yet to be convinced of the girl's innocence.

"According to Marjorie's story, Miss Archer," began Mrs. Dean with gentle directness, "she has been the victim of circumstantial evidence. I am not here to criticize your stand in this affair. I understand that you must have been severely tried. I merely wish to ask you to allow Marjorie to tell her story from beginning to end. She came to me yesterday with it, and asked my advice. I deferred decision until to-day. It seems I was a day too late. However, I wish her to do the explaining."

A faint, embarrassed flush stole to Miss Archer's face as she listened. She was beginning to realize that she had for once been too quick to condemn. Mrs. Dean was too high-principled a woman to attempt to smooth over her own child's offences. Under the battery of her friend's clear eyes, the principal found herself penitently responding: "Mrs. Dean, I must admit that I am at fault. Had I stopped to listen to Marjorie, I am now certain that I should have found her explanation satisfactory."

"Thank you." Mrs. Dean extended a gracious hand in which the principal laid her own with a smile. The two women understood each other perfectly.

Marjorie's sensitive lips quivered as Miss Archer's hand went out to her also. "I am only too glad to be able to apologize for misjudging you, Marjorie," she said with grave gentleness. "The truest atonement which I can make is to say 'I believe in you' without a hearing."

"But I wish to tell you everything, Miss Archer," assured Marjorie earnestly. "It was only because I hated the idea of tale-bearing that I didn't tell you this morning. I thought that Miss Farnham——"

"Would tell me," supplemented the principal. "I quite understand. Frankly it would help me very much if you put me in complete possession of the facts of the case. I hardly believe you owe it to Miss Farnham to conceal anything."

With a charitable striving toward placing the other girl in the least obnoxious light, Marjorie gave Miss Archer a true but unmalicious version of all that had passed between herself and Rowena Farnham.

"This is simply outrageous," was Miss Archer's emphatic verdict. "Miss Farnham is a menace to Sanford High School. In all my experience with young women I have never met with her equal. I shall recommend the Board that she be not allowed to enter the school. A firebrand such as she has shown herself to be is more than likely to spread her devastating influence throughout the school. We have a duty to perform to the parents who intrust their daughters to us which cannot be overlooked."

"I agree with you," was Mrs. Dean's grave response. "Still, I am very sorry for this girl, and for her parents. We all wish to be proud of our children. It must be dreadful to be disappointed in them."

"You, at least, will never be called upon to bear such a disappointment." Miss Archer's hearty reply caused an exchange of affectionate glances between her hearers.

"I hope I shall always prove worthy of Captain's and your trust." Marjorie's little speech rung with modest sincerity. Hesitatingly she added: "Miss Archer, couldn't you possibly give Miss Farnham another chance? When I was at her house the other day she said that her father and mother wanted her to go to high school. She'd rather go to boarding school, but they won't let her. If she isn't allowed to enter Sanford High she will have to go away to school. That might not be the best thing for her." Marjorie paused, blushing at her own temerity.

"You are a very forgiving little girl." Miss Archer eyed the pleader in a whimsical fashion. "There is a great deal in your view of the matter, too. It is a question of one girl's parents against many, however. So far as I can remember this is the first case in the history of the school that warranted dismissal. As you have been the chief sufferer in this tangle, your plea for clemency should be respected. It shall be mentioned to the members of the Board of Education. That is all I can promise now. Personally, as you are great-spirited enough to plead for her, I am willing to do my part. But only on your account. I doubt the advisability of allowing her to go on with her examinations. However, 'forewarned is forearmed.' Should she be permitted to enter the school, I shall keep a watchful eye on her."

Real admiration of Marjorie's readiness to help one who had treated her so shabbily caused the principal to speak as confidentially to her pupil as she might have to a member of the Board. Marjorie, as well as her mother, was aware of this. Yet far from being elated at the mark of confidence, the pretty junior bore her honors almost humbly. She merely thanked Miss Archer in the sweet, gracious fashion that set her apart from all other girls with whom the principal had come in contact during her long service on the field of education.

Almost immediately afterward the Deans said farewell and departed happily to convey the good news to their somewhat impatient chauffeur, who sat in the automobile pondering whimsically on the length and breadth of women's chats. Long after they had gone, Marjorie's winsome, selfless personality haunted the busy principal. To be truly great one must be truly good was her inner reflection. Remembering past circumstances in which Marjorie had figured ever as a force for good, she marveled that she could have doubted her. And as a vision of the girl's lovely face, animated by the light from within, rose before her she mentally prophesied that Marjorie Dean was destined one day to reach the heights.

CHAPTER IX—A SUDDEN ATTACK

"Where were you yesterday afternoon?" demanded Jerry Macy, as Marjorie walked into the locker room at the close of the morning session.

Marjorie considered for a moment. Should she tell Jerry or should she not? She decided in the negative. "I was at home a part of the afternoon."

Jerry measured her with a calculating eye. "You don't want to tell me, do you?" was her blunt question. "All right. Forget it. Anyway, we missed you. You're a mysterious person. One day you march off on a dark, secret errand after making lavish promises to treat on the next. When that day rolls around you don't appear at all. Never mind. I saved your face by treating for you." Jerry delivered her opinion of her friend's peculiar behavior good-humoredly enough. Underneath, however, she was a tiny bit peeved. She was very fond of Marjorie and prided herself that she was entirely in the latter's confidence.

"You're not cross with me, are you, Jerry?" Marjorie regarded the stout girl rather anxiously. She could not conceive of being on the outs with funny, bluff Geraldine Macy.

"No; I'm not a silly like Mignon," mumbled Jerry gruffly. "You ought to know that by this time without asking me."

"Jerry Macy, I believe you are angry with me," declared Marjorie, looking still more troubled.

"No, I'm not," came the quick retort. "I'm not blind, either, and my head isn't made of wood."

"What do you mean?" It was Marjorie's turn to speak quickly.

"Just what I say," asserted Jerry. "You've had some sort of trouble over that Farnham girl. Rowena—humph! It ought to be Row-ena with a special accent on the Row. I knew by the way you looked and spoke of her day before yesterday that something had gone wrong. I'll bet I know where you went on that errand, too. You went to her house. Now didn't you?"

Marjorie gave a short laugh. It held a note of vexation. "Really, Jerry, you ought to be a detective. How did you know where I went yesterday after I left you?"

"Oh, I just guessed it. It's like you to do that sort of thing. I'm dying to hear what it's all about. Are you going to tell me now?" She accented the "now" quite triumphantly.

"I hadn't intended to mention it to anyone, but I might as well tell you. You seem to know quite a little bit about it already. I can't say anything more now. Here come Susan and Muriel. We'll talk of it after we leave them at their street. By the way, where is Constance? She wasn't in school this morning."

"Don't know. I wondered about her, too. She didn't say yesterday that she wasn't coming to school to-day. Maybe her father marched into Gray Gables without notice."

"Perhaps. I'll ask the girls if they know."

Neither Susan, Muriel nor Irma, the latter joining the quartette immediately after, knew the reason for Constance Stevens' absence. The five girls trooped out of the building together, chatting gaily as they started home for luncheon. Marjorie gave a little shiver as it occurred to her how near she had come to losing her right to be a pupil of Sanford High. She felt that nothing save the loss of her dear ones would have hurt her more than to have been dismissed from school under a cloud.

"Now tell me everything," began Jerry, the moment they had parted from the three girls to continue on up the pleasant, tree-lined avenue.

"I think that was simply awful," burst forth the now irate Jerry, as Marjorie concluded her narration. "Talk about Mignon—she's an angel with beautiful feathery wings, when you come to compare her with Row-ena. I hope the Board says she can't set foot in school again. That's what I hope. I'll tell my father to vote against letting her try any more examinations. That's what I'll do."

"You mustn't do that." Marjorie spoke with unusual severity. "What I've said to you is in confidence. Besides, it wouldn't be fair. For her father's and mother's sake I think she ought to have another chance. It might be the very best thing for her to go to high school. She will be far better off at home than away at boarding school. If she could go away to a college it would be different. Colleges are more strict and dignified. A girl just has to live up to their traditions. General says that even in the most select boarding schools the girls have too much liberty. So you see it wouldn't be a good place for this girl."

"I see you're a goose," was Jerry's unflattering comment. "You're a dear goose, though. You certainly have the reform habit. I can tell you, though, that you are all wrong about this Farnham girl. You remember how beautifully we reformed Mignon, and how grateful she was. Mignon's a mere infant beside gentle, little Row-ena. You notice I still say Row. It's a very good name for her. Of course, we could change off occasionally and call her Fightena, or Quarrelena, or Scrapena." Jerry giggled at her own witticism.

Marjorie could not forbear joining her. Jerry's disapproval of things was usually tinged with comedy. "You're a heartless person, Jeremiah," she reproved lightly. "I'm not going to try to reform Miss Farnham. I can't imagine her as taking kindly to it. I'm only saying that she ought to have another chance."

"Well, if you can stand it I can," Jerry sighed, then chuckled as her vivid imagination pictured to her the high-handed Rowena struggling in the clutches of reform. "Miss Archer ought to have thought twice and spoken once," she added grimly. "That's what she's always preaching to us to do." Jerry was no respecter of personages.

"I can't blame her much," Marjorie shook her head. "It's dreadful to think that someone you've trusted is dishonorable. It hurts a good deal worse than if it were someone you had expected would fail you. I know."

"I suppose you do." Jerry understood the significant "I know." Rather more gently she continued: "Perhaps you're right about Fightena, I mean Rowena. You generally are right, only you've got into some tangled webs trying to prove it. Anyway, she won't be a junior if she does manage to get into school. She'll be a sophomore. I hope she stays where she belongs. You'd better look out for her, though. If she really thinks you wrote that anonymous letter—I don't believe she does—she'll try to get even. With Mignon La Salle to help, she might bother you a good deal. I hope they have a falling out."

"You are always hoping some terrible thing," laughed Marjorie. "You have the hoping habit, and your hopes about other people are really horrifying."

"Never mind, they never amount to much," consoled Jerry with a chuckle. "I've been hoping awful things about people I don't like for years and that's all the good it's ever done."

"I think I'll run over to Gray Gables after school," Marjorie changed the subject with sudden abruptness. "Want to go with me?"

"I'll go," assented Jerry. "I owe Charlie a box of candy. I promised it to him the night of Mary's farewell party. Mary wrote me a dandy letter. Did I tell you about it?"

"No. I've had one from her, too; eighteen pages."

"Some letter. Mine was only ten."

The introduction of Mary's name into the conversation kept the two girls busy talking until they were about to part company.

"Don't forget you are going with me to see Constance," reminded Marjorie as Jerry left her at the Macys' gate.

"Do you believe that I could possibly forget?" Jerry laid a fat hand over her heart in ridiculous imitation of a certain sentimental high school youth whom Marjorie continually endeavored to dodge.

"See that you don't," was her laughing retort. "Shall we ask Muriel, Susan and Irma to go with us?"

"None of them can go. Muriel has to take a piano lesson. Susan has a date with her dressmaker, and Irma's going shopping with her mother. You see I know everything about everybody," asserted Jerry, unconsciously repeating Constance Stevens' very words.

"You surely do," Marjorie agreed. "Good-bye, then. I'll meet you in the locker room after school to-night."

"My name is Johnny-on-the-spot," returned the irrepressible Jerry over her shoulder.

"Oh, dear!" Marjorie exclaimed in impatience, as she walked into the locker room at the end of the afternoon session to find Jerry already there ahead of her. "I've left my Cæsar in my desk. I'll have to go back after it. That lesson for to-morrow is dreadfully long. Somehow I couldn't keep my attention on study that last hour, so I just bundled all my books together and thought I'd put in a busy evening. I don't see how I missed my Commentaries. It shows that my mind was wandering."

"Come on over to my house this evening. You can use my Cæsar. We'll put one over on the busy little bee and have some fun afterward. Besides, Hal will be grateful to me for a week. I'll make good use of his gratitude, too," grinned wily Jerry.

Marjorie's cheeks grew delightfully pink. In her frank, girlish fashion she was very fond of Jerry's handsome brother. Although her liking for him was not one of foolish sentimentality, she could not help being a trifle pleased at this direct insinuation of his preference for her.

"All right. I'm sure Captain will say 'yes,'" she made reply. "I won't bother to go back after my book. If I did Miss Merton might snap at me. I try to keep out of her way as much as I can. Where are the girls? Have they gone?"

"Yes, they beat it in a hurry. Come on. Let's be on our way." Though deplorably addicted to slang, Jerry was at least forcefully succinct.

It was a fairly long walk to Gray Gables, but their way led through one of the prettiest parts of Sanford. Situated almost on the outskirts of the town, the picturesque dwelling was in itself one of the beauty spots of the thriving little city.

"There's the Jail." Jerry indexed a plump finger toward the inhospitable stone house which Marjorie had so lately visited. The two girls had reached the point where a turn in the wide, elm-shaded avenue brought them within sight of the La Salle and Farnham properties. "It would be a good place for Row-ena, if she had to stay locked up there. She could think over her sins and reform without help. I hope——"

"There you go again," laughed Marjorie. "Don't do it. Suppose some day all these things you have hoped about other people were to come back to you."

"I won't worry about it until they do," Jerry made optimistic answer. "If I——" She checked herself to stare at a runabout that shot past them, driven at a reckless rate of speed by an elfish-faced girl. "There they go!" she exclaimed. "Did you see who was in that machine? Oh, look! They're slowing up! Now they've stopped! I hope they've had a breakdown."

Marjorie's eyes were already riveted on the runabout which they were now approaching. A tall figure whom she at once recognized as belonging to Rowena Farnham was in the act of emerging from the machine. Hatless, her auburn head gleaming in the sun, her black eyes flaming challenge, she stood at one side of the runabout, drawn up for battle.

"She's waiting for us!" gasped Jerry. "Let's turn around and walk the other way, just to fool her. No; let's not. I guess we can hold our own."

"I shall have nothing to say to her," decided Marjorie, a youthful picture of cold disdain. "Don't you say a word, either, Jerry. We'll walk on about our own business, just as though we didn't even see her."

Jerry had no time to reply. Almost immediately they caught up with the belligerent Rowena. Realizing that her quarry was about to elude her, she sprang squarely in front of them with, "Wait a minute. I've something to say to you." The "you" was directed at Marjorie.

Marjorie was about to circle the lively impediment and move on, when Mignon La Salle called from the runabout, "I told you she was a coward, Rowena." A scornful laugh accompanied the insult.

That settled it. Marjorie's recent resolution flew to the winds. "I will hear whatever you have to say," she declared quietly, stopping short.

"I don't very well see how you can do anything else," sneered Rowena. "I suppose you think that you gained a great deal by your tale-bearing yesterday, don't you? Let me tell you, you've made a mistake. I'm going to be a sophomore in Sanford High School just the same. You'll see. You are a sneaking little prig, and I'm going to make it my business to let every girl in school know it. You can't——"

"You can't talk like that to Marjorie Dean." Before Marjorie could reply, Jerry Macy leaped into a hot defense. "I won't have it! She is my friend."

"Shh! Jerry, please don't," Marjorie protested.

"I will. Don't stop me. You," she glared at Rowena, "make me sick. I could tell you in about one minute where you get off at, but it isn't worth the waste of breath. Marjorie Dean has more friends in a minute in Sanford High than you'll ever have. You think you and Mignon La Salle can do a whole lot. Better not try it, you'll wish you hadn't. Now get busy and beat it. You're blocking the highway."

"What a delightful person you are," jeered Rowena. "Just the sort of friend I'd imagine Miss Dean might have. As I have had the pleasure of telling her what I think of her, you may as well hear my opinion of yourself. You are the rudest girl I ever met, and the slangiest. My father and mother would never forgive me if they knew I even spoke to such a girl." Having delivered herself of this Parthian shot, Rowena wheeled and stepped into the runabout with, "Go ahead, Mignon. I don't care to be seen talking with such persons."

As the runabout started away with a defiant chug, Jerry and Marjorie stared at each other in silence.

"I hope——" began Jerry, then stopped. "Say," she went on the next instant, "that was what Hal would call a hot shot, wasn't it?"

"It was," Marjorie admitted. In spite of her vexation at the unexpected attack, she could hardly repress a smile. Quite unknowingly Rowena had attacked Jerry's pet failing. Her constant use of popular slang was a severe cross to both her father and mother. Over and over she had been lectured by them on this very subject, only to maintain that if Hal used slang she saw no reason why she shouldn't. To please them she made spasmodic efforts toward polite English, but when excited or angry she was certain to drop back into this forceful but inelegant vernacular.

"I suppose I do use a whole lot of slang." Jerry made the admission rather ruefully. "Mother says I'm the limit. There I go again. I mean mother says I'm—what am I?" she asked with a giggle.

"You are a very good friend, Jerry." Marjorie looked her affection for the crestfallen champion of her rights. "I wouldn't worry about what she—Miss Farnham says. If you think you ought not to use slang, then just try not to use it." Marjorie was too greatly touched by Jerry's loyalty to peck at this minor failing. "What a strange combination those two girls make!" she mused. "I can't imagine them being friends for very long. They are both too fond of having their own way. I must say I wasn't scared by all those threats. It isn't what others say about one that counts, it's what one really is that makes a difference."

"That's just what I think," agreed Jerry. "We all know Mignon so well now that we can pretty nearly beat her at her own game. As for this Rowena, she'd better wait until she gets back into Sanford High before she plans to do much. All that sort of thing is so silly and useless, now isn't it? It reminds me of these blood-and-thunder movies like 'The Curse of a Red Hot Hate,' or 'The Double-dyed Villain's Horrible Revenge,' or 'The Iron Hand of Hatred's Death-Dealing Wallop.'" Jerry saw fit to chuckle at this last creation of fancifully appropriate title. "You're right about those two, though. Don't you remember I said the same thing when I first told you of this Farnham girl? Mignon has met her match, at last. She'll find it out, too, before she's many weeks older, or my name's not Jerry Macy."

CHAPTER X—A CRUSHING PENALTY

As Jerry had guessed, Constance Stevens' absence from school was due to the fact that her foster-father had descended upon Gray Gables for a brief visit. He was delighted to see both Marjorie and Jerry. Constance insisted that they should remain to dinner, whereupon the tireless telephone was put into use and the two remained at Gray Gables, there to spend a most agreeable evening. At about eleven o'clock Hal Macy appeared to take them home in the Macy's smart limousine. Thus, in the pleasure of being with her friends, Marjorie quite forgot the disagreeable incident that had earlier befallen herself and Jerry. Strange to say, Cæsar's Commentaries, also, faded from recollection, and it was not until they were driving home that the estimable Roman was tardily remembered along with previous good intentions. "It's unprepared for ours," was Jerry's doleful cry, thereby proving that the will to abolish slang was better than the deed.

Due to placing pleasure before duty, Marjorie felt it incumbent upon her to make an early entrance into school the next morning for the purpose of taking a hasty peep at her neglected text books. She was lucky, she told herself, in that the last hour in the morning would give her an opportunity to go over her Cæsar lesson. She, therefore, confined her attention to her English literature, deciding that she could somehow manage to slide through her French without absolute failure. Civil government would also have to take its chance for one recitation.

When at fifteen minutes past eleven she came into the study hall from French class and settled herself to begin the business of Latin, she was for once glad to lay hold on the fat, green volume devoted to the doings of the invincible Cæsar. Opening it, a faint cluck of surprise fell from her lips as she took from it a square, white envelope addressed to herself. It was unsealed and as she drew forth the folded paper which it held she wondered mightily how it had come to be there. She was very sure she had not placed it in the book. Her bewilderment deepened as she read:

"Miss Dean:

"After what occurred the other day in the principal's office it is surprising that you were not expelled from Sanford High School. It proves you to be a special pet of Miss Archer. Such unfairness is contemptible in a principal. It should be exposed, along with your dishonesty. Sooner or later even that will be found out and you will receive your just deserts. It is a long lane that has no turning.

"The Observer."

Marjorie emitted a faint sigh of pure amazement as she finished reading this sinister prediction of her ultimate downfall. It was a piece of rank absurdity, evidently penned by someone who had no intimate knowledge of inside facts. Still it filled her with a curious sense of horror. She loathed the very idea of an anonymous letter. Once before since she had first set foot in Sanford High the experience of receiving one of these mysterious communications had been hers. It had pertained to basket ball, however. She had easily guessed its origin and it had troubled her little. This letter was of an entirely different character. It proved that among the girls with whom she daily met and associated there was one, at least, who did not wish her well.

As she reread the spiteful message, her thoughts leaped to Rowena Farnham as the person most open to suspicion. Yet Rowena had made a direct attack upon her. Again there was Mignon. She was wholly capable of such a deed. Strangely enough, Marjorie was seized with the belief that neither girl was responsible for it. She did not know why she believed this to be true. She simply accepted it as such, and cudgelled her brain for another more plausible solution of the mystery.

As she studied it the more she became convinced that the writing was the same as that of the similarly signed letter Miss Archer had received. The stationery, too, was the same. The words, "The Observer," were the crowning proof which entirely exonerated Rowena. She had certainly not written the first note. Therefore, she had not written the second. Marjorie was in a quandary as to whether or not she should go frankly to the principal and exhibit the letter. She felt that Miss Archer would wish to see it, and at once take the matter up. She could hardly charge Rowena with it, thereby lessening her chances of entering the school. This second note made no mention of Rowena. Its spitefulness was directed entirely toward Marjorie herself. As it pertained wholly to her, she believed that it might be better to keep the affair locked within her own breast. After all, it might amount to nothing. No doubt, Rowena had related her own version of the algebra problem to Mignon. Mignon was noted for her malicious powers of gossip. A garbled account on her part of the matter might have aroused some one of her few allies to this cowardly method of attack. Still this explanation would not cover the writing of the first letter.

Quite at sea regarding its source, Marjorie gave the distasteful missive an impatient little flip that sent it fluttering off her desk to the floor. Reaching down she lifted it, holding it away from her as though it were a noisome weed. She burned to tear it into bits, but an inner prompting stayed her destroying hands. Replacing it in the envelope, she tucked it inside her silk blouse, determining to file it away at home in case she needed it for future reference. She hoped, however, that it would never be needed. Whoever had slipped it into her Cæsar must have done so after she had left her desk on the previous afternoon, following the close of the session. She wished she knew those who had lingered in the study hall after half-past three. This she was not likely to learn. Her own intimate friends had all passed out of the study hall at the ringing of the closing bell. She resolved that she would make casual inquiries elsewhere in the hope of finding a clue.

During the rest of the week she pursued this course with tactful assiduousness, but she could discover nothing worth while. What she did learn, however, was that due to a strenuous appeal to the Board of Education on the part of Mr. Farnham, his daughter had been allowed, on strict promise of future good behavior, to try an entirely new set of examinations. Fortune must have attended her, for on the next Monday she appeared in the study hall as radiantly triumphant as though she had received a great honor, rather than a reluctant admission into the sophomore fold.

"Well, she got there!" hailed Jerry Macy in high disgust, happening to meet Marjorie in the corridor between classes on the morning of Rowena's retarded arrival. "My father said they had quite a time about it. She got into school by just one vote. He wouldn't tell me which way he voted, but he said he was glad she wasn't his daughter."

"I'm honestly glad for hers and her parents' sake that she was allowed another trial." Marjorie spoke with sincere earnestness. "She's had a severe lesson. She may profit by it and get along without any more trouble."

"Profit by nothing," grumbled Jerry. "She can't change her disposition any more than a cat can grow feathers or an ostrich whiskers. Row-ena, Scrapena, Fightena, Quarrelena she is and will be forever and forever. Let's not talk about her. She makes me—I mean I feel somewhat languid whenever her name is mentioned." Jerry delivered her polite emendation with irresistible drollery. "Did you know that there's to be a junior basket ball try-out next Tuesday after school?"

"No." Marjorie's interest was aroused. "Who told you? It certainly hasn't been announced."

"Ellen Seymour told me. She's going to help Miss Davis manage the team this year in Marcia Arnold's place. I imagine she'll do most of the managing. I guess Miss Davis had enough of basket ball last year. She told Ellen that it took up too much of her time. She knew, I guess, that the upper class girls wouldn't relish her interference. Ellen says you must be sure to be at the try-out. She hopes you——" Jerry left off speaking and looked sheepish.

"Well, why don't you finish? What does Ellen wish me to do?"

"You'll find out at the try-out. Now don't ask me any more questions about it." Jerry's cheerful grin belied her brusque words.

"You're a very tantalizing person," smiled Marjorie. "There goes the second bell. I'll see you later." She scudded away, wondering what it was that Jerry had stoutly refused to reveal. Evidently, it must be something of pleasant import, else Jerry would have frowned rather than smiled.

The next day, directly after opening exercises, Miss Merton dryly read out the official call to the try-out. It was received by the junior section with an audible joy which she sternly quenched. Miss Merton was in even less sympathy with "that rough-and-tumble game" than she was with the girls who elected to play it. It was directly due to her that Miss Davis had lost interest in it.

To those intimately interested in making the junior team, the Tuesday afternoon session seemed interminable. Eager eyes frequently consulted the moon-faced study-hall clock, as its hands traveled imperturbably toward the hour of reprieve. Would half-past three never come? At ten minutes past three Muriel Harding's impatience vented itself in the writing of a heart-felt complaint to Marjorie. She wrote:

"This afternoon is one hundred years long. Darling Miss Merton wishes it was two hundred. The very idea that we are going to the try-out gives her pain. She hates herself, but she hates basket ball worse. If I should invite her to the try-out she would gobble me up. So I shall not risk my precious self. You may do the inviting."

This uncomplimentary tribute to Miss Merton was whisked successfully down the section and into Marjorie's hands. As note-passing was obnoxious to the crabbed teacher, Muriel had neither addressed nor signed it. She had craftily whispered her instructions to the girl ahead of her, who had obligingly repeated them to the next and so on down the row. Unfortunately, Miss Merton's eyes had spied it on its journey. She instantly left her desk to pounce upon it at the moment it was delivered into Marjorie's keeping.

"You may give me that note, Miss Dean," she thundered, extending a thin, rigid hand.

"Pardon me, Miss Merton, but this note is for me." Her fingers closing about it, Marjorie lifted resolute, brown eyes to the disagreeable face above her.

"Give it to me instantly. You are an impertinent young woman." Miss Merton glared down as though quite ready to take Marjorie by the shoulders and shake her.

Back in her own seat, Muriel Harding was divided between admiration for Marjorie and fear that she would yield to Miss Merton's demand. Despite lack of signature, the latter would have little trouble in identifying the writer were she given a chance to read the note. Muriel saw trouble looming darkly on her horizon.

"I am sorry you think me impertinent. I do not mean to be." The soft voice rang with quiet decision. "But I cannot give you this note." Marjorie calmly put the note in her blouse, and, folding her hands, awaited the storm.

"You will stay here to-night until you give it to me," decreed Miss Merton grimly. Beaten for the time, she stalked back to her desk, quite aware that she could hardly have imposed a more crushing penalty. True, her effort to obtain the note had been fruitless, but one thing was patent: Marjorie Dean would not be present at the junior basket ball try-out.

CHAPTER XI—AT THE ELEVENTH HOUR

Left to herself for a brief respite, Marjorie drew out the note and read it. An expression of amused consternation flashed into her eyes as she took in its spirit. Knowing the writing to be Muriel's she was now glad she had stood her ground. Note writing was not forbidden in Sanford High and never had been. Miss Merton alone, of all the teachers, strenuously opposed it. To be sure, it was not regarded by them with special favor. Nevertheless, in the class-rooms no one was ever taken to task for it unless it seriously interfered with the recitation. Marjorie did not know Miss Archer's views on the subject, but she believed her principal too great-minded to cavil at such trifles.

The instant she had finished reading the note, she reduced it to unreadable bits, leaving them in plain sight on her desk. Not by so much as a backward glance did she betray the writer. Knowing Miss Merton to be on the alert, she took no chances. Should the latter send her to Miss Archer, she would very quickly express herself on the subject. As a junior she believed that the time for treating her as a member of the primary grade had long since passed.

It was not until she had effectually blocked all possibility of the note falling into Miss Merton's possession that she remembered the try-out. Her heart sank as she recalled what a lengthy, lonely stay in the study hall meant. The try-out would go on without her. She would lose all chance of obtaining a place on the junior team. Her changeful face paled a trifle as she sadly accepted this dire disaster to her hopes. If only Muriel had not written that note.

The first closing bell sent a tremor of despair to her heavy heart. She wondered how long Miss Merton would detain her. She had said, "You will stay here to-night until you give it to me." Even in the midst of misfortune the edict took a humorous turn. She had a vision of herself and Miss Merton keeping a lonely, all-night vigil in the study hall.

At the second bell the long lines of girls began a decorous filing down the aisles to the great doors. Marjorie watched them go, vainly pondering on why, thus far, her junior year had been so filled with mishaps. A bad beginning sometimes made a good ending was her only comforting reflection. She hoped that in her case it would prove true.

"Why are you staying, Miss Harding?" rasped forth Miss Merton when the big room had at last emptied itself.

Marjorie faced about with a start. She had not reckoned on this. She made a desperate sign to Muriel to go. Muriel merely shook an obstinate head. Then she announced bravely, "I wrote that note to Miss Dean."

"Then you may remain in your seat," snapped the frowning teacher. "Miss Dean, do you intend to give me that note?"

"I have destroyed it," came the calm reply.

"You are determined to defy me, I see. Very well, you may tell me the contents of it. I saw you read it after I had returned to my desk."

"I have nothing to say," Marjorie replied with terse obstinacy.

"Miss Harding, you may tell me what you wrote." Miss Merton suddenly swung her attack from Marjorie to Muriel.

"I will not." Muriel spoke with hot decision. "Neither Miss Dean nor I are grammar school children. I see no reason why we should be treated as such. I think it very ridiculous, and I will not submit to it. You may send me to Miss Archer if you like. I am quite ready to say to her what I have just said to you."

As Muriel's challenge of defiance cut the storm-laden atmosphere, a most unexpected thing happened. Almost as if the mere mention of her name had served to bring her to the scene, Miss Archer walked into the study hall. She had come in time to catch Muriel's last sentence, and her quick faculties had leaped to conclusion.

"What is it that you are quite ready to say to me, Miss Harding?" was her grave interrogation.

Miss Merton's sallow cheeks took on a lively tinge of red. She was not specially anxious to bring Miss Archer into the discussion. Had the recipient of the note been other than Marjorie Dean, she would have allowed the incident to pass with a caustic rebuke. But her dislike for the winsome girl was deep-rooted. She could never resist the slightest opportunity to vent it publicly.

"I wrote a note to Miss Dean, Miss Archer," burst forth Muriel. "Miss Merton asked Miss Dean for it and she wouldn't give it to her. So Miss Merton said she must stay here until she did. Miss Dean tore the note up. I stayed because I wrote it. Miss Merton says we must tell her what was in that note. I won't do it. Neither will Marjorie. I just said that I did not think we ought to be treated like grammar school children. I said, too, that I would be willing to say so to you, and I have."

Miss Archer's quizzical gaze traveled from Muriel's flushed face to Marjorie's composed features. Here was, indeed, a problem in that unknown quantity, girl nature. Miss Archer was too thoroughly acquainted with the ways of girls not to comprehend what lay beneath this out and out defiance of Miss Merton's commands. She understood, if Miss Merton did not, or would not, the rather overdrawn sense of school-girl honor which prompted the rebellion. She knew that except in extreme cases, there was little to be obtained by using force. It was all too likely to defeat its own object.

"The attitude of these two young women toward me is insufferable." Miss Merton now took up a harsh stand. She did not intend the principal should allow the matter to be passed over lightly. "Miss Dean, in particular, has been most disrespectful. In fact, ever since she became a pupil of this school she has derived an especial delight from annoying me."

Miss Archer's face wore an inscrutable expression as she listened. Years of association with Miss Merton had taught her to read between the lines. Yet she knew she must now proceed with the utmost diplomacy. As a teacher Miss Merton was entitled to the respect of her pupils. She had an inner conviction, however, that the irate woman was piling injustice upon Marjorie's shoulders. She herself was beginning to understand the girl's motives could never be classed as unworthy. Young in years, she possessed already a breadth of mind which Miss Merton could never hope to attain.

"You are entitled to the utmost respect on the part of your pupils, Miss Merton," she levelly acknowledged. "I am sorry to hear bad reports of any of my pupils. I am sure that Miss Harding and Miss Dean will rectify the matter with an apology. As for the note, perhaps it might be wiser to allow the matter to drop."

"Girls," she now addressed the belligerents, "it seems to me that, as long as note-writing has proved a source of trouble to you, you might better give up the practice. Let me ask you a question. Was there any grave and important reason for writing that note?"

Muriel Harding hung her head. "No, Miss Archer," came her low answer.

Marjorie's pale face took on a faint glow of pink. "It was not necessary," she admitted.

"Very well. You have both agreed that it was unnecessary. My advice to you is to discontinue the practice. I must insist that both of you make apology to Miss Merton for the annoyance you have caused."

"Miss Merton, I regret that you should have been annoyed by me." Marjorie made an immediate and dignified apology, which was perfectly sincere on her part. For more reasons than one she deplored the annoyance.

Muriel, however, hesitated a second or two before committing herself. Suddenly it dawned upon her that Miss Archer's demand for apology had a deeper significance. She thereupon made haste to repeat Marjorie's exact words.

Miss Merton received both apologetic speeches in black silence. She was inwardly furious with the principal, not only for her unexpected intrusion, but for the lax manner in which she had administered discipline. At least, Miss Merton considered it distinctly lax. Still, she knew that it would be in bad taste to try to overrule the principal's decision. "You are dismissed," she said stiffly. "See to it that you conduct yourselves properly hereafter." She could not resist this one touch of authority.

The ex-culprits lost no time in leaving the study hall behind them. Not a word passed between them until the door of the junior locker room had closed upon them. Their eyes meeting, they burst into laughter, discreetly subdued, but most expressive of their feelings. Each mind held the same thought. What would Miss Merton have said had she read the note?

CHAPTER XII—A DOUBTFUL VICTORY

"Marjorie Dean, you are true blue!" exclaimed Muriel. "Whatever possessed me to write that awful note? If Miss Merton had read it—well, you can guess what would have happened. I shook in my shoes when I heard her ask you for it."

"I'm glad I didn't give it to her." An angry sparkle leaped into Marjorie's soft eyes. "She only made a fuss about it because it was I who had it. I think Miss Archer understood that. I love her for it. She treats us always as though we were young women; not as naughty children. But we mustn't stand here. It's four o'clock now. I am afraid we won't have a chance to play. Only about fifteen or twenty juniors are going to try for the team. It may be made already." Marjorie picked up the bag which contained her basket ball suit and tennis shoes.

"Let us hustle along then," urged Muriel. Seizing her friend by one hand, her luggage in the other, the two raced for the gymnasium, hoping against hope.

"It's all over." Muriel cried out in disappointment as they entered the great room.

"I am afraid so," faltered Marjorie, as she noted the group of bloomer-clad girls standing idle at one end of the gymnasium. Here and there about the floor were others in uniform. Altogether she counted eighteen. Ellen Seymour and two other seniors were seated on the platform, their chairs drawn together, their attention apparently fixed on a pad on Ellen's knee. Spectators had been firmly but politely denied admission. Ellen had pronounced them a detriment to the try-out and elected that they should remain away.

"Hello, Marjorie Dean," joyfully called out Harriet Delaney. As she hailed Marjorie she ran toward the two girls. "We thought you were lost to us forever. Where were you, Muriel? You surely didn't have to stay."

"Did you make the team?" was Muriel's excited query.

"Not yet." Harriet's eyes twinkled. "The try-out hasn't begun yet."

"Hasn't begun!" echoed two voices.

"No. Ellen was awfully cross about the way Miss Merton acted, so she said we'd wait for Marjorie. Then, when Muriel didn't appear, she said, that if neither of you materialized, she would have the try-out put off until to-morrow. Miss Davis is so busy with that new system of gymnastics she's going to adopt this year that she's left basket ball to Ellen. I don't see how she could help herself, though. Last year the juniors and seniors ran their own teams."

"Ellen's a dear," exulted Muriel. "We are lucky to have her for manager. Marjorie and I will be her grateful slaves for the rest of the year. I wrote that note; so, naturally, I had to stay and face the music."

"You did!" It was Harriet who now registered surprise. "What was in it?"

Muriel giggled. She could now afford to laugh. "Oh, a lot of sweet things about Miss Merton. You can guess just how sweet they were."

"Goodness!" breathed Harriet. "No wonder Marjorie wouldn't give it up. She—why, she's gone!"

Marjorie had stopped only to greet Harriet. While Muriel was explaining matters, she slipped away to the platform where Ellen Seymour sat. "It was splendid in you, Ellen!" she burst forth, as she reached the senior's side. "Thank you, ever so much."

"Hurrah! Here's Marjorie." Ellen sprang up, her pleasant face breaking into a smile. "I'm so glad you came at last, and so sorry for what happened. You must tell me how you came out. But not now. We shall have to hustle to make up for lost time. I suppose you know Miss Elbert and Miss Horner. No?" Ellen promptly performed introductions.

"Pleased to meet you," nodded both young women. Neither looked specially delighted. Miss Elbert, a small, plump girl with near-sighted, gray eyes, bowed in reserved fashion. Miss Horner, a rather pretty brunette, acknowledged the introduction with languid grace. Marjorie had long known both by sight. On two different occasions she had been introduced to Miss Horner. Afterward, on meeting her in the street, the latter had made no sign of recognition.

"I suppose you are satisfied now, Ellen," drawled Miss Horner sweetly. "You are lucky, Miss Dean, to have Ellen for a champion. She insisted that we must wait for you."

"I am very grateful to her," Marjorie made courteous reply. Had there lurked a touch of sarcasm in the other's polite comment?

"Miss Merton is altogether too fussy," remarked Miss Elbert. Her blunt tone quite belied her reserved nod. "She tried that with me last year. It didn't work, though." Her air of constraint vanished in a bright glance, which indicated friendliness.

"You must remember that she has a great deal to try her," reminded Miss Horner softly.

Again Marjorie thought she sensed hostility. She laid it to the supposition that Miss Horner was, perhaps, a trifle peevish at being delayed. Yet she could not resist the quiet comment, "Miss Merton is also very trying."

"Of course she is," agreed Ellen warmly. "You know it as well as we do, Charlotte Horner. You have no cause to love her. Just remember how cranky she was to you during your freshman year."

"That was a long time ago," shrugged the senior. "I understand her much better now than then." The placid answer held a suspicion of condescending approval of Miss Merton.

"I'm glad someone does," flung back Ellen with careless good humor. "Hurry along, Marjorie, and get into your basket ball suit. I shouldn't have kept you talking." Drawing her aside, she whispered: "I'd rather see you play center on the team than any girl I know."

"It seems to me, Ellen," drawled Charlotte Horner, as her indolent gaze followed Marjorie across the floor to the dressing room, "that you are babying that Miss Dean entirely too much. Someone told me the other day that she has a bad attack of swelled head. I must say, I think her self-opinionated. She answered me very pertly."

"If you mean her remark about Miss Merton, she only spoke the truth," defended Ellen hotly, completely astonished by this unexpected attack on Marjorie. "She is not in the least self-opinionated nor vain. It's remarkable that she isn't. She is very pretty and awfully popular."

"Glad you told me," murmured the other, lazily unbelieving. "I know several girls with whom she is not particularly popular."

To this Ellen made no response. With vexation at her own stupidity, she now remembered too late that Charlotte Horner had always been rather friendly with Mignon La Salle. Remembering only Charlotte's undeniable prowess as a basket ball player, she had asked her to act with herself and Leila Elbert as one of the three judges at the try-out. This explained why Charlotte had not been in favor of postponing the try-out in case Marjorie were detained indefinitely. Ellen found herself hoping that personal prejudice would not influence Charlotte to decry Marjorie's work on the floor.

"I think Miss Dean is very nice." It was Leila Elbert who made this announcement. Her reserved manner had arisen merely from shyness. She was a quiet, diffident girl, who, beyond an enthusiasm for basket ball, had mixed little with the social side of high school. She was an expert player who had been on the same team with Ellen during her freshman, sophomore and junior years. Accordingly, she was eminently fitted to judge the merits of the respective contestants.

"That's sweet in you." Ellen flashed her a grateful look. It would be two against one in Marjorie's favor.

Within ten minutes after seeking the dressing room Marjorie issued from it ready for the fray, wearing her sophomore basket ball uniform. Running up to Ellen she announced: "I am ready. So is Muriel." In a lower tone she added: "It was dear in you to wish me well." Then she trotted over and joined the contestants, who had gradually collected in one spot.

"All right." Ellen left the platform and approached the fruitful material for junior honors. "Girls," she began, with an elaborate bow, "behold your stern manager."

She was interrupted by giggling applause. Cheerful Ellen Seymour was beloved throughout Sanford High School.

"Much obliged," she nodded gaily. "As I was saying when interrupted by your heart-felt appreciation, I am your manager. This year there will be no senior team. The seniors have soared to heights beyond mere basket ball. I had to soar with them, though I wasn't in a soaring mood. Since I can't play the good old game alone, I've decided to bury my disappointment in managership. Of course, you know that you can't all play. So if you're not chosen, don't be disappointed. It's going to be an absolutely fair try-out. If you're chosen, it is because you are a better player than the girl who isn't. Now please line up until I count you over."

It was a nondescript line that whipped itself promptly into position. There were the five gray-clad girls who had made up Mignon La Salle's famous team. There were also the five black-garbed players who had comprised Marjorie's squad. Besides these were ten new applicants in blue gymnasium suits who had not been fortunate enough to make either of the two teams that had striven against each other in the sophomore year. These girls had decided to try again, hoping that better luck would be theirs.

Marjorie thrilled with excitement as she cast a quick glance up and down the line. Every face was set in determined fashion. It was going to be much harder than ever before to make the team.

Ellen Seymour walked up and down the row of girls with the air of a general. She was shrewdly calculating the best plan of action. It would hardly be fair to try out the black and scarlet girls against the grays, leaving the other ten of lesser experience to play against each other. Among the new girls there was, undoubtedly, some excellent material which contact with the regular players was sure to bring out. She, therefore, chose five blues to play against two grays and three black and scarlet girls. Mignon and Daisy Griggs represented the grays, Marjorie, Susan and Harriet Delaney the black and scarlet.

Clearing the floor of the others, Ellen signaled the two teams to their places and soon had the ball in play. It seemed very strange to Marjorie to find herself once more on the same team with Mignon La Salle. She was too busy attending to her own affairs, however, to give it more than a passing thought. Centering her whole mind on her work she played with her usual snap and brilliancy.

After twenty minutes' energetic work, the warning whistle sounded retreat. Then the other ten girls remaining were ordered to the floor to show what they could do. When, after the same allowance of time, they had been called off, the three judges went into consultation with the result that ten names were struck from the list Ellen held. These names Ellen read out, expressing a regret for the failure of their owners to make good that was in a measure quite consoling. They left the floor to their more fortunate sisters apparently with the best possible grace, considering the disappointment that was theirs.

There were still left Susan, Muriel, Marjorie, Mignon, Daisy Griggs and Anne Easton of the seasoned teams. The other were four of the blue-clad girls who had done surprisingly well. These ten were again divided into opposing fives and went at it with a will.

T-r-ill! Ellen's whistle at last called an end to the spirited fray. The girls pattered off the playing floor. Grouped together they breathlessly awaited the verdict.

This time it was longer in coming. Up on the judge's stand, Ellen Seymour found herself participating in the wrangle with Charlotte Horner, which she had anticipated. But Marjorie was not alone subject of it. It was Mignon's basket ball future, too, that now tottered. Four names had been struck off the list of ten. It lay between Mignon and Marjorie Dean as to whom the fifth should be.

"Mignon is a better player than this Dean girl," sharply argued Charlotte Horner. "But poor Mignon simply wasn't up to her usual form to-day."

"But it's to-day that counts, else why have a try-out?" protested Ellen. "Marjorie has completely outplayed her in this last test. I consider Marjorie the better player at any time. She is reliable. Mignon isn't. I insist that Marjorie shall have the position. I think she's the best player of the whole team."

"And I insist that Mignon must have it." In her anger Charlotte forgot her usual languid drawl.

"It rests with Leila." Ellen shrugged her shoulders. "What is your opinion, Leila?"

"Miss Dean is the better player," declared Leila stolidly. "Anyone can see that."

"Two against one. The ayes have it." Ellen drew a firm pencil through Mignon's name.

And thus Marjorie Dean won a victory over Mignon La Salle, which was destined to bring her a great deal of unhappiness.

CHAPTER XIII—UNSEEN; UNKNOWN; UNGUESSED

Outside the school building Jerry Macy and Irma Linton were holding a patient vigil. Not permitted to witness the try-out they had declared their intention of waiting across the street for their friends. Confidently expecting that their wait would be long, they had set off for Sargent's directly after school, there to while away at least a part of the time. It was twenty minutes after four when they returned to the school and determinedly perched themselves upon the top step of the long flight where they proposed to remain stationed until the try-out should be over. As ardent fans, they had a lively curiosity to know as soon as possible the results of the contest. They were also deeply concerned as to what had transpired between Marjorie and Miss Merton.

"Good gracious!" grumbled Jerry, as she frowningly consulted her wrist watch. "When do you suppose it will be over? It's half-past five now. I hope——"

"Hark!" Irma raised a warning hand. "I hear voices. Here they come at last."

As she spoke the heavy door behind her swung open. One after another the contestants began issuing forth to unite into little groups as they passed down the steps to the street. Jerry and Irma were now on their feet eagerly watching for their friends. Jerry's shrewd power of observation had already been put to good use. Thus far she glimpsed defeat in the faces of those who passed. Among them was Mignon La Salle. Her arm linked in that of Charlotte Horner, the French girl was carrying on a low-toned monologue, the very nature of which could be read in the stormy play of her lowering features.

Jerry gave Irma a significant nudge as Mignon switched past them without sign of recognition. Irma nodded slightly to show that she understood its import. She, too, had guessed that Mignon had not made the team.

"At last!" Jerry sighed relief, as Marjorie stepped across the threshold, followed by Susan, Muriel and Daisy Griggs. "What's the good word?" She hailed.

"We are the real people," boasted Muriel Harding, a throbbing note of triumph in her light tones. "Marjorie, Susan, Daisy and I made the team. The fifth girl is Rita Talbot. She was the only one of the blues chosen. Poor Harriet didn't make it. Neither did Esther. Harriet's been chosen as a sub, though. So has that queer little green-eyed Warner girl. She's such a quiet mouse, I never even dreamed she could play basket ball. She can, though." Muriel rattled off all this, hardly stopping to take breath.

"So dear Miss Merton changed her mind," burst forth Jerry irrelevantly. "How long did she keep you, Marjorie? What did she say?" They had now progressed as far as the sidewalk and had halted there to talk.

Marjorie entered into brief details, giving Muriel the lion's share of credit for her blunt explanation to Miss Archer. "If Muriel hadn't spoken so plainly, Miss Archer might not have seen things in the right light," she ended.

"Don't you believe it," disagreed Jerry. "Miss Archer knows Miss Merton like a book. It's a real comfort to have a principal like her. Say, I'll bet Mignon is so mad she can't see straight. You should have seen her when she passed us. She was talking a blue streak to that Miss Horner. She was one of the judges, wasn't she?"

"Yes." Marjorie's face clouded at mention of the languidly spoken senior. It now occurred to her that she had not been at fault in believing that Charlotte Horner disliked her. No doubt Mignon was the motive for her dislike. Like Ellen, she, too, tardily recalled that the two had been occasionally seen together last year. It might account also for the emphatic wagging of heads that had gone on among the three judges before the final result of the try-out had been announced.

"I suppose you are going to play the sophomores." Irma's soft intonation brought Marjorie out of her brown study.

"Of course." It was Daisy Griggs who answered. "They are to have their try-out to-morrow afternoon. I don't believe we will be ready to play them before November. We have a lot of practice ahead of us. We'll have to have new suits, too. But we won't know until we have a meeting what colors to choose. We ought to ask the subs what they'd like. We can't very well go by the junior colors this year. They are deep crimson and white, you know. We couldn't possibly have white suits with a crimson J, and crimson suits wouldn't be pretty, either."

"I think they would," put in Muriel Harding stoutly. "We could have our suits of a little darker crimson than the class color. They would be stunning with a white J on the blouse and a wide, rolling collar of white broadcloth. Besides, crimson is a victorious color. We'd just have to win. It would be inspiring."

"It sounds good to me," approved Susan. "They'd certainly be different from any we've ever had. We could all put together and buy the cloth. Then have them made by one person instead of each going to our own dressmaker."

"I think that would be nice," nodded Marjorie. "But we want to please Daisy, too, so perhaps——"

"Oh, I don't mind. Just so they aren't a glaring red," hastily amended Daisy. "I suppose the subs will want to have new suits, too. We ought to call a meeting of the team some time this week. That reminds me, we don't know yet who is to be captain. You ought to be, Marjorie. I think Ellen will ask you."

"No." Marjorie shook a decided head. "To be given center is honor enough for me. Girls, I'd love to have Muriel for captain. She'd be simply splendid."

"Oh, no, not me," protested Muriel in ungrammatical confusion. Nevertheless, she flushed with pleasure at Marjorie's generous proposal.

"That would be fine," asserted Susan Atwell heartily. She was not in the least jealous because Marjorie had not proposed her for the honor. She had long since learned that Marjorie Dean was incapable of showing favoritism. She had selected Muriel strictly with the good of the team in mind.

"Let's ask Ellen if we can't have Muriel," said Daisy Griggs earnestly.

"You see three of us are of the same mind," Marjorie pointed out with a smile. "I know Rita will say so, too. But where are she and Harriet?"

"Still in the gym, I guess, with Ellen. Harriet lives next door to Ellen," reminded Susan. "They'll be along presently."

"I can't wait for them," Marjorie demurred. "It's almost six. Captain will wonder why I'm so late. Come on, Jerry and Irma," she called. Jerry and Irma had wandered a little away from the group and were deeply engaged in earnest discussion. "How many of you are going our way?"

"I'm going to my aunt's for dinner," said Muriel. "So I'll say good-bye. Daisy goes my way, too. See you to-morrow. Come along, Daisy."

Left to themselves, Susan, Marjorie, Irma and Jerry swung off toward home, four abreast.

"See here, Marjorie," began Jerry. "You want to look out for Mignon. I told you how mad she looked when she passed us. Irma saw, too. She'll try to do something to get you off the team and herself on. See if she doesn't."

"I'm not going to bother my head about her," Marjorie made careless reply. "She has never really hurt anyone she's tried to hurt since I've known her. With Ellen Seymour managing the teams, we are all sure of fair play."

"Don't be too sure," muttered Jerry. She added in a louder tone, "Ellen's not much protection with Mignon on the job. If she can't play, she'll try to fix it so somebody else can't. Not you, perhaps. Anyway, it won't do any harm for you to keep your eyes open."

"Don't croak, Jeremiah." Marjorie laid a playful hand on Jerry's lips. "Didn't I tell you long ago that I should not allow Mignon La Salle to trouble me this year? I am going to keep at a safe distance from her."

"I hope you stick to that," was Jerry's ungracious retort. Under her breath she added, "but I doubt it."

Jerry Macy's well-meant warning was destined, however, to come back most forcibly to Marjorie no later than the following morning. As she ran down the steps of her home and on down the walk on her way to school, she encountered the postman at the gate. He handed her two letters, which she received with a gurgle of girlish delight. On the top envelope she had glimpsed Mary's familiar script. The gurgle changed to a dismayed gasp as she examined the other. Only too quickly had she recognized the handwriting. Shoving Mary's letter into the pocket of her pretty tan coat, she hastily opened the other envelope. Her evil genius had again come to life. A wave of hot resentment swept her as she unfolded the one sheet of heavy white paper and read:

"Miss Dean:

"No doubt you think yourself very clever to have made the junior team. You could never have done so had partiality not been shown. Others at the try-out were much more worthy of the choice. You believe because you can dress like a doll and are popular with a few rattle-brained girls that everyone likes you. But you are mistaken. A few persons, at least, know how vain and silly and deceitful you are. You pretend to hate snobbery, but you are a snob. Some day everyone will know you for what you really are. The time is not far off. Beware.

"The Observer."

Turning, Marjorie went slowly back to the house and climbed the stairs to her room. Pausing before her desk, she opened it. From a pigeon-hole she extracted another letter. Carefully she compared it with the one that had come by post. Yes, they must have both emanated from the same source. Stationery, writing and signature were unmistakable proofs. With a sigh she shoved them both into the pigeon-hole. Who could her mysterious enemy be? These letters were certainly of the variety she had heard classed as "poison pen."

Thus far she had flouted the idea of Mignon La Salle as the writer of them. Now she was forced to wonder if she had been wrong. Was it possible that Mignon had lurked outside Miss Archer's office on the morning when she had solved the problem for Rowena Farnham? If this were so, the letter Miss Archer had received might then be accredited to her, as well as the two now in her desk. Barring Rowena Farnham, Marjorie knew no one else who would be likely to engage in such a despicable enterprise. If Mignon were guilty of this, Jerry Macy's warning had not been an idle one. It, therefore, behooved her, Marjorie Dean, to be on her guard. Yet how could she guard herself against a shadow, an enemy unseen; unknown; unguessed?

CHAPTER XIV—A SOLDIER IN EARNEST

Absorbed in a vain attempt to find a clue to the mysterious prophesier of evil, Marjorie forgot Mary Raymond's letter until she happened to thrust a hand into her coat pocket on the way home from school at noon. Mary's long, cheery epistle partially atoned for the hateful sentiments expressed by the unknown. On her return home in the afternoon, a second comforter was accorded her in a letter from Constance Stevens. The day after Marjorie and Jerry had spent the evening at Gray Gables Mr. Stevens had gone to New York. Constance had accompanied him.

Since the great change had taken place in the girl's life her school days had been more or less broken. Still she managed to keep up in her classes despite frequent short absences from school. It was tacitly understood, not only by Miss Archer, but also by Constance's other teachers, that she intended to study for a grand opera début as soon as her high school days were over. The mere possession of so remarkable a voice as was hers rather set her apart in some indefinite fashion from her schoolmates. Where others would have been taken to strict account for absence, she was allowed an unusual amount of consideration. Undoubtedly, the fact that when actually in school she invariably acquitted herself with credit in her various studies had much to do with the leniency accorded her. From a very humble person, she was rapidly becoming a personage from whom Sanford expected one day to hear great things.

Marjorie Dean felt Constance's absences more keenly than anyone else. She had been particularly lonesome for her friend during this latest one, and the news that Constance would return to Sanford and to school on the following week banished for the time the shadow of the morning's unpleasant incident.

"Constance will be home on Sunday, Captain," she caroled gleefully, as she danced about the living room by way of expressing her jubilation.

"I am glad to hear it. You really need the child to cheer you up. You've been looking rather solemn lately, my dear. Aren't you happy in your school? Sit down here and give an account of yourself," commanded Mrs. Dean with a smile.

"Oh, yes." The answer was accompanied by a faint sigh, as Marjorie curled up on the floor beside her mother. "So far, this has been rather a queer year, though. Nothing very pleasant has happened except basket ball. That's always a joy. Our team is doing beautifully. We are to play the sophomores on the Saturday before Thanksgiving. It's going to be a real tussle. Ellen

Seymour says there are some great players among the sophs. You'll come to the game, Captain?"

"I suppose I must. You consider me a loyal fan. That means I must live up to my reputation. By the way, Lieutenant, did that girl who made you so much trouble enter high school? You never told me."

"You mean Rowena Farnham? Yes; she was allowed to try another set of examinations. Jerry Macy said she won the chance by only one vote. Jerry's father's a member of the Board. I wouldn't tell anyone else but you, though, about that one vote. She is a sophomore now. I see her in the study hall, but we never speak. The girls say she is quite popular with the sophs. I suppose she's trying hard to make up her lost ground." Marjorie's inflection was slightly bored. She felt that she had small cause for interest in Rowena. She had never told her mother of the latter's attack on herself and Jerry. She preferred not to think of it, much less talk of it. To her it had seemed utterly senseless, as well as cheap.

"And how is Mignon La Salle doing?" questioned Mrs. Dean. "I haven't heard you mention her, either. I must say I am very glad that you and she are not likely to be thrown together again. Poor little Mary made a bad mistake last year. It is wonderful that things ever worked out as well as they did." Mrs. Dean's face grew stern as she recalled the tangle in which Mary's obstinacy had involved her daughter.

"Oh, Mignon has found a friend in Rowena Farnham. They go together all the time. Jerry says they will soon fall out. I am sure they are welcome to chum together, if they choose." Marjorie shrugged her shoulders as though desirous of dismissing both girls from her thoughts.

"Jerry is quite likely to be a true prophet," commented Mrs. Dean. "She is a very wise girl, but decidedly slangy. I cannot understand why a girl brought up in her surroundings should be so thoroughly addicted to slang."

"She's trying awfully hard not to use it." Recalling Jerry's recent efforts to speak more elegant English, Marjorie laughed outright. "She's so funny, Captain. If any other girl I know used slang as she does, I wouldn't like it. But Jerry! Well, she's different. Next to Connie and Mary I love her best of all my friends. I don't know what I'd do without her."

"She is a very fine girl, in spite of her brusque ways," praised Mrs. Dean. "General is fond of her, too." She added this little tribute lest Marjorie might feel that she had been unduly critical. She understood the fact that Marjorie's friends were sacred to her and on that account rarely found fault with them. Marjorie could be trusted to choose her associates wisely. Those to whom her sympathies went out usually proved themselves worthy of her regard. Motherly anxiety alone had prompted Mrs. Dean to draw her daughter out with a view toward learning the cause of Marjorie's recent air of wistful preoccupation. Daily it had become more noticeable. If a repetition of last year's sorrows threatened her only child, Mrs. Dean did not propose to be kept in the dark until it became well-nigh impossible to adjust matters.

Secretly Marjorie was aware of this anxiety on her mother's part. She felt that she ought to show her Captain the sinister letters she had received, yet she was loath to do so. Her mother's inquiry concerning Mignon had caused her to reflect uneasily that now if ever was the moment for unburdening her mind. "Captain," she began, "you know that something is bothering me, don't you?"

"Yes. I have been hoping you would tell me." Mrs. Dean laid an encouraging hand on the drooping, brown head against her knee.

"Wait a minute." Imbued with a desperate energy, Marjorie sprang to her feet and ran from the room. She soon returned, the disturbing letters clutched tightly in one hand. "I wish you to read these," she said. Tendering them to her mother, she drew up a chair opposite Mrs. Dean and sat down.

Silence hung over the cheerful room while Mrs. Dean acquainted herself with the cause of Marjorie's perturbation. Contempt filled her voice as she finally said: "A most despicable bit of work, Lieutenant. The writer had good reason to withhold her true name. So this explains the solemn face you have been wearing of late. I wouldn't take it very deeply to heart, my dear. Whoever wrote these letters must possess a most cowardly nature."

"That's just what I think," nodded Marjorie. "You see it really started with the letter Miss Archer received. You know, the one about the algebra problem. The only person I can really suspect of writing any of them is Mignon. But she's not this sort of coward. Besides, I don't believe she'd write just this kind of letter. What sort of person do you think would, Captain?"

Before answering, Mrs. Dean thoughtfully reread both letters. "It is hard to say," she mused. "It looks to me as though the writer of them might have been prompted by jealousy. The second one in particular is full of jealous spite. I suppose you don't care to let Miss Archer see them."

"No." Marjorie shook a vehement head. "I'd rather worry through without that. Perhaps there won't be any more of them. I hope not. Anyway, I'm glad I told you about them. If another does come, I can bring it to you and not feel so bad over it as if I had to think things out alone. Even if I knew this very minute who wrote them, I don't know what I'd do about it. It would depend upon who the girl was, whether or not I'd say anything to her. It's all very mysterious and aggravating, isn't it?" she added wistfully.

"It's far worse than that." Mrs. Dean's lips set in a displeased line. "Sanford High School appears to harbor some very peculiar girls. I can't imagine any such thing happening to you at Franklin High. I don't like it at all. If the rest of your junior year is going to be like this, you might better go away to a good preparatory school."

"Oh, Captain, don't say that!" Marjorie cried out in distress. "I couldn't bear to leave you and General and Sanford High. I'd be terribly unhappy away from home. Please say you didn't really mean that." Tears lurked in her pleading tones.

"Now, now, Lieutenant," came the soothing reply, "don't be so ready to run out to meet calamity. I only suggested your going away as a means of taking you out of these pits you seem always innocently to be tumbling into. You know that General and I could hardly get along without our girl. It is of your welfare I am thinking."

Marjorie slipped to her mother's side and wound coaxing arms about her. "I was afraid this would hurt you. That's why I hated to tell you. Don't worry, Captain. Everything will come out all right. It always has, you know. So long as I keep a clear conscience, nothing can really hurt me. I hope I'm too good a soldier to be frightened, just because I've been fired upon by an unseen enemy. If I ran away now I'd be a deserter, and a deserter's a disgrace to an army. So you see there's only one thing to do; stand by and stick fast to my colors. I've got to be a soldier in earnest."

CHAPTER XV—AN UNWILLING FOLLOWER

Marjorie's confidential talk with her Captain brought to her a renewal of faith in herself, which carried her along serenely through various small difficulties which continually sprang up in her junior path. One of them was Miss Merton, who seemed always on the watch for an opportunity to belittle the girl she so detested. Still another was the hostile interest Mignon La Salle had again begun to take in her. Hardly a day passed without an angry recital on Jerry's part of something she had heard against Marjorie, which had originally come from Mignon or Rowena Farnham. Mignon's ally, Charlotte Horner, was an equal source for provocation. Although she had no special right to do so, she often dropped in on junior basket ball practice merely to find food for adverse criticism of Marjorie. She watched the latter with a hawk-like eye, only to go forth and make capital of any small imperfection in Marjorie's playing, which she saw or fancied she saw.

The fact that Rowena Farnham was a member of the sophomore team did not add to Marjorie's happiness. She had no wish to come into such close contact with her, which the approaching games between the two teams would necessitate. From Jerry, the indefatigable news-gatherer, she had learned that Rowena was a skilful, but rather rough player. Knowing her to be utterly without scruple, Marjorie had small reason to believe she could be trusted to play an absolutely fair game against her opponents. Rowena was already becoming an insolent power in the sophomore class. Her extreme audacity, coupled with her good looks and fine clothes, brought her a certain amount of prestige in Sanford High School. She possessed to a marked degree that impudent quality of daring, which is so peculiarly fascinating to school girls.

Although she was not sincerely liked she was admired and feared. She had a fund of clever sayings at her command, which gave her a reputation for brilliancy. The frequent reproof of her teachers rolled off her like water from a duck's back. She made public sport of whomever she pleased, whenever it pleased her to do so, with a conscienceless air of good humor that rendered her a dangerous foe. She never hesitated to forge her way to whatever she wanted, in a hail-fellow-well-met manner which changed like a flash to insolence with the slightest opposition offered. She was a bully of the first water, but with the glamor of her newness still upon her, the worst side of her nature was yet to be revealed to many.

Marjorie Dean and Jerry Macy, at least, entertained no illusions concerning her. Neither did Mignon La Salle. For once in her life, Mignon was beginning to find herself completely overshadowed by a nature far more hatefully mischievous than her own. True she was Rowena's most intimate friend. Yet there were times when she inwardly regretted having rushed blindly into such a friendship. Striving ever to rule, now she was invariably overruled. Instead of being leader, she became follower. Rowena criticized, satirized and domineered over her, all in the name of friendship. Had she been anyone else, Mignon would not have borne long with her bullying. She would have speedily put an end to their association. Rowena, however, was one not thus easily to be dropped. In Mignon she glimpsed powers for mischief-making only secondary to her own. She preferred, therefore, to cling to her and was clever enough never to allow Mignon's flashes of resentment against her high-handedness to mature into open rebellion. Those who knew the French girl for exactly what she was agreed that Mignon had at last met her match. They also agreed that a taste of her own medicine would no doubt do her a great deal of good.

The approach of Thanksgiving also brought with it a stir of excitement for the coming basket ball game, the first to be played in a series of four, which were scheduled to take place at intervals in the school year. The sophomore team had already played the freshman and given them a complete whitewashing. Now they were clamoring to meet the juniors and repeat their victory. The junior team had attended the freshman-sophomore game in a body, thereby realizing to the full the strength of their opponents. Reluctantly, they were forced to admit the brilliancy of Rowena Farnham as a player. She knew the game and she went into it with a dash and vigor that marked her as a powerful adversary. Naturally, it won her an admiration which she determined should grow and deepen with each fresh achievement.

Her doughty deeds on the floor of contest merely imbued the junior team with stronger resolution to win the coming game. They practised with stubborn energy, sedulously striving to overcome whatever they knew to be their weak points. Though manager of all the teams, Ellen Seymour's heart was secretly with them. This they felt rather than knew. Outwardly, Ellen was impartial. She made them no show of favoritism, but they divined that she would rejoice to see them win. There was no doubt of the smoothness of their team work. Having played basket ball on the freshman and sophomore teams, Marjorie Dean herself knew that the squad of which she was now a member excelled any other of past experience. Fairly confident that it could hold its own, she looked impatiently forward to the hour of action.

To set one's heart too steadfastly on a particular thing, seems sometimes to court disappointment. On the Thursday before the game an unexpected state of affairs came to pass. It started with a notice on the bulletin board requesting the presence of the junior team in the gymnasium at four o'clock that afternoon. It was signed "Ellen Seymour, Manager." Naturally, the juniors thought little of it. They were accustomed to such notices. Ellen, no doubt, had some special communication to make that had to do with them. But when five minutes after four saw them gathered in the gymnasium to meet their manager, her sober face warned them that the unusual was afoot.

"Girls, I have something to ask of you which you may not wish to do. I am not going to urge you to do it. You are free to choose your own course. As it especially concerns you, yours is the right to decide. Two girls of the sophomore team are ill. Martha Tyrell has come down with tonsilitis, and Nellie Simmons is threatened with pneumonia. Both are in bed. They can't possibly play on Saturday. The sophs are awfully cut up about it. They wouldn't mind using one sub, but two, they say, is one too many. They have asked me to ask you if you are willing to postpone the game until these girls are well again."

"I don't see why we should," objected Captain Muriel Harding. "I don't believe they'd do the same for us. Of what use are subs, if not to replace absent players?"

"That's what I think," put in Daisy Griggs. "It's too provoking. Everyone is looking forward to the game. If we don't play we'll disappoint a whole lot of people. It's very nervy in the sophs to ask us to do such a thing. Besides, we are crazy to wear our new suits."

Ellen smiled quizzically. "Remember, you are to do as you please about it," was all she said, betraying neither pleasure or displeasure at the ready protests.

"I suppose the sophomores will think us awfully mean if we don't do as they ask," ventured Rita Talbot.

"Oh, let them think," declared Susan Atwell impatiently. "It's the first time I ever heard of such a thing. They must be terribly afraid we'll beat them."

"That's just the point." At this juncture Marjorie broke into the discussion. "If we insist on playing and win, they might say we won because we had them at a disadvantage. That wouldn't be much of a victory, would it?"

"That's so." Muriel reluctantly admitted the force of Marjorie's argument. "I know at least one of them who would say just that."

"Mustn't be personal," gently chided Ellen. Nevertheless, there was a twinkle in her blue eyes. The sophomore who had come to her had insinuated what

Marjorie had voiced. "I'll give you ten minutes to talk it over. I promised to let the sophomores know to-night. The girl who came to me is waiting in the senior locker room for your answer."

"I'm ready to decide now," asserted Marjorie. "For my part I'm willing to postpone the game."

"We might as well," conceded Captain Muriel ruefully. Marjorie's point had gone home. "If we win we want it to be a sweeping victory."

One by one the three other interested parties agreed that it seemed best to yield gracefully to the plea.

"Now that you've all spoken I'm going to tell you my opinion," announced Ellen. "I am glad that you are willing to do this. It becomes you as juniors. No one can say that you have been anything but strictly generous. You deserve a crown of victory for being so nice about this."

Ellen's conclusion brought a smile to five faces. Her remark might be construed as a declaration of favor toward them.

"I believe you'd love to see us win the whole four games, Ellen Seymour," was Muriel's frank comment.

"As your august manager, my lips are sealed," Ellen retorted laughingly. "Now I must leave you and put an anxious sophomore out of her misery. While you are waiting for the sick to get well you can put in some more practice." With this injunction she left them.

Once out of the gymnasium, her smile vanished. The anxious sophomore was Rowena Farnham. Ellen cherished small liking for this arrogant, self-centered young person whose request had been more in the nature of a command. Personally, she had not favored putting off the game. Had illness befallen a member or members of any team on which she had formerly played, no such favor would have been asked. Nothing short of incapacitation of the whole squad would have brought forth a stay in activities. Yet as manager she was obliged to be strictly impersonal. True, she might have exercised her authority and herself made the decision. But she had deemed the other way wisest.

On entering the senior locker room she was still more annoyed to find Mignon La Salle with Rowena. If Ellen disliked the latter, she had less love for the tricky French girl. "Birds of a feather," she mentally styled them as she coldly bowed to Mignon. Her chilly recognition was not returned. Mignon had not forgiven her for the try-out.

"Well, what's the verdict?" inquired Rowena, satirically pleasant. Her manner toward dignified Ellen verged on insolence.

"The junior team are willing to postpone the game," informed Ellen briefly. She intended the interview to be a short one.

"They know on which side their bread is buttered," laughed the other girl. "I suppose they weren't specially delighted. Did they make much fuss before they gave in?"

"As I have delivered my message, I will say 'good afternoon,'" Ellen returned stiffly.

"Don't be in too much of a hurry," drawled Rowena. "When I ask a question, I expect an answer."

"Good afternoon." Ellen wheeled and walked calmly from the locker room. Rowena's expectations were a matter of indifference to the disgusted manager. She, at least, was not to be bullied.

Mignon La Salle laughed unpleasantly. "You were foolish to waste your breath on her." She wagged her black head in the direction of the door, which had just closed behind Ellen. "You didn't impress her that much." She snapped her fingers significantly.

Smarting under the dignified snubbing Ellen had administered, Rowena hailed Mignon as an escape valve. "You keep your remarks to yourself," she blustered. "How dare you stand there laughing and snapping your fingers? No wonder people say you're two-faced and tricky. You're so deceitful you don't know your own mind. One minute you come whining to me about this Seymour snip, the next you take sides with her."

"I wasn't standing up for her and you know it," muttered Mignon. As always, Rowena's brutally expressed opinion of herself had a vastly chastening effect on the designing French girl. Rowena never minced matters. She delivered her remarks straight from the shoulder, indifferent to whether they pleased or displeased. Mignon's disregard for sincerity and honor suited her admirably. She was equally devoid of these virtues. Mignon made an excellent confederate. Still, she had to be kept in her place. Her very love of subtle intrigue made plain speaking abhorrent to her. On occasions when Rowena mercilessly held before her the mirror of truth, she invariably retired in confusion. At the same time she entertained a wholesome respect for the one who thus dared to do it. This explained to a great extent the strong influence which Rowena exerted over her. She was not happy in this new friendship. More than once she had meditated ending it. Fear of the other's furious retaliation was a signal preventative. Rowena, as a friend, was greatly to be preferred to Rowena as an enemy.

As she sulkily viewed the Titian-haired tyrant, who knew her too well for her own peace of mind, she wondered why she had not flung back taunt for taunt. Perhaps Rowena made a shrewd guess regarding her thoughts. Adopting a milder tone she said brusquely: "Oh, quit pouting and come along. None of these stupid girls are worth quarreling over. I suppose that Marjorie Dean, the big baby, told Miss Seymour something hateful about me. That's the reason she acted so frosty."

At the mere mention of Marjorie's name Mignon's elfish face grew dark. She and Rowena had at least one bond in common, they both despised Marjorie Dean. Mignon reflected that no scheme she had devised for humbling the former had ever borne lasting fruit. Rowena might succeed where she had failed. Rowena had sworn reprisal for the affair of the algebra problem. Undoubtedly, she would seize upon the first opportunity for retaliation. With such a glorious prospect ahead of her, Mignon craftily decided to stick to Rowena and share in her triumph.

CHAPTER XVI—A TINY CLUE

The end of the week following Thanksgiving brought the two temporarily disabled sophomore basket ball players back to school. The day after their return a notice appeared on the bulletin board stating that the junior-sophomore game would be played on the next Saturday afternoon. From all sides it received profound approbation and the recent postponement of the contest served to give it greater importance. The sophomore team had been highly delighted with the respite, and gratefully accorded the credit to Rowena Farnham, who reveled in her sudden advance in popularity.

The juniors had little to say to the world at large. Among themselves they said a great deal. One and all they agreed that the victory of the coming game must be theirs. They yearned to show the public that in postponing the game they had merely postponed the glory of winning it. Though they knew the strength of the opposing team, they confidently believed themselves to be even stronger. How it happened, none of them were quite able to explain, but when the fateful hour of conflict arrived the victor's crown was wrested from them. A score of - in favor of the sophomores sent them off the field of defeat, crestfallen but remarkably good-natured, considering the circumstances.

Behind the closed door of their dressing room, with the jubilant shouts of the sophomores still ringing in their ears, they proceeded to take stock of themselves and their triumphant opponents.

"There is no use in talking, that Rowena Farnham is a wonderful player," was Muriel Harding's rueful admission. "She could almost have won the game playing alone against us."

"She's a very rough player," cried Daisy Griggs. "She tears about the floor like a wild Indian. She gave me two or three awful bumps."

"Still, you can't say she did anything that one could make a fuss about," said Rita Talbot slowly. "I guess she's too clever for that."

"That's just it," chimed in Susan Atwell crossly. "She's as sharp as a needle. She goes just far enough to get what she wants without getting into trouble by it. Anyway, they didn't win much of a victory. If that last throw of Marjorie's hadn't missed the basket we'd have tied the score. It's a pity the game ended right there. Three or four minutes more were all we needed."

"I was sure I'd make it," declared Marjorie rather mournfully, "but a little before, in that big rush, I was shoved forward by someone and nearly fell. I made a slide but didn't quite touch the floor. All my weight was on my right arm and I felt it afterward when I threw the ball."

"Who shoved you forward? That's what I'd like to know," came suspiciously from Susan. "If——"

"Oh, it wasn't anyone's fault," Marjorie hastened to assure her. "It was just one of those provoking things that have to happen."

"Listen to those shrieks of joy," grumbled Muriel, as a fresh clamor began out in the gymnasium. "Oh, why didn't we beat them?"

"Never mind," consoled Marjorie. "There'd be just as much noise if we had won. You can't blame them. Next time it will be our turn. We've still three more chances. Now that we've played the sophs once, we'll know better what to do when we play them again. We really ought to go out there and congratulate them. Then they would know that we weren't jealous of them."

"I'd just as soon congratulate a big, striped tiger as that Rowena Farnham. She makes me think of one. She has that cruel, tigerish way about her. Ugh! I can't endure that girl." Muriel Harding made a gesture of abhorrence.

"Come in," called Marjorie as four loud knocks beat upon the door. "It's Jerry, Connie and Irma," she explained, as the door opened to admit the trio.

"Better luck next time," cheerfully saluted Jerry Macy. "You girls played a bang-up, I mean, a splendid game. I was sure you'd tie that score. You had a slight accident, didn't you, Marjorie?"

"Yes. Did you notice it?" Marjorie glanced curiously at Jerry's imperturbable face.

"I always notice everything," retorted Jerry. "I hope——"

Marjorie flashed her a warning look. "It wasn't anything that could be avoided," she answered with a finality that Jerry understood, if no one else did. "I move that we go down to Sargent's and celebrate our defeat," she quickly added. "Have a seat, girls. It won't take us long to get into our everyday clothes."

"Such a shame," bewailed Daisy Griggs. "After we've gone to the trouble of having these stunning suits made, then we have to be robbed of a chance to parade around the gym as winners. Anyway, they're a whole lot prettier than the sophs' suits. I didn't like that dark green and blue they had as well as ours."

"They stuck to the sophomore colors, though," reminded Rita. "It's a wonder that Rowena Farnham didn't appear in some wonderful creation that had nothing to do with class colors. It would be just like her."

Despite their regret over losing the game, the defeated team, accompanied by Jerry, Constance, Irma and Harriet Delaney, who afterwards dropped in upon them, set off for the all-consoling Sargent's in fairly good humor, there to spend not only a talkative session, but their pocket money as well.

It was not until Jerry, Constance and Marjorie had reluctantly torn themselves from their friends to stroll homeward through the crisp December air that Jerry unburdened herself with gusto.

"Marjorie Dean," she began impetuously, "do you or don't you know why you nearly fell down in that rush?"

"I know, of course," nodded Marjorie. "Someone swept me forward and I almost lost my balance. It's happened to me before. What is it that you are trying to tell me, Jerry?"

"That someone was Row-ena," stated Jerry briefly. "Isn't that so, Connie?"

"It looked that way," Connie admitted. "I thought she played very roughly all through the game."

"If it were she, I don't believe she did it purposely," responded Marjorie. "Even if she did, I'm not going to worry about it. I rather expected she might. Mignon used to do that sort of thing. You remember what a time we had about it last year. But her team and ours were concerned in it. That's why I took it up. As it was only I to whom it happened this time, I shall say nothing. I don't wish to start trouble over basket ball this year. If I spoke of it to Ellen she would take it up. You know what Rowena Farnham would say. She'd declare it was simply a case of spite on my part. That I was using it only as an excuse for not being able to throw that last ball to basket. Then she'd go around and tell others that we were whining because we were beaten in a fair fight. I might better say nothing at all. The only thing for us to do is to keep our own counsel and win the next game."

"I guess your head is level," was Jerry's gloomy admission. She was as much distressed over their defeat as were the juniors themselves.

"Marjorie's head is always level," smiled Constance Stevens. "I am almost certain that you girls will win the next game. Luck just happened to be with the sophomores to-day. I don't think they work together as well as you. Miss Farnham is a much better player than the others. Still, I imagine that she might not always do so well as she did in this game. If she saw that things were going against her, she would be quite likely to get furiously angry and lose her head." Quiet Constance had been making a close study of Rowena during the game. Raised in the hard school of experience, she had considerable insight into character. She seldom criticized openly, but when she did, her opinions were received with respect.

"Your head's on the same level plane with Marjorie's, Connie," agreed Jerry. "I think, too, that Rowena Farnham would be apt to make blunders if she got good and mad. Speaking of getting mad reminds me that Lucy Warner is pouting about those suits of ours. She told Harriet to-day that she thought they were simply hideous. Harriet said that she wouldn't go in with you girls when you ordered them. She considered them a waste of money. Said if she had one, she'd never get a chance to wear it. Pleasant young person, isn't she?"

"Perhaps she couldn't afford to have one," remarked Constance thoughtfully. "You know her mother is a widow and supports the two of them by doing plain sewing. I imagine they must be quite poor. They live in a tiny house on Radcliffe Street, and Lucy never goes to even the high school parties, or to Sargent's, or any place that costs money. She is a queer little thing. I've tried ever so many times to be nice to her, but she always snubs me. Maybe she thinks I'm trying to patronize her. I can't help feeling sorry for her. You see I know so well what it means to be very poor—and proud," ended Constance, flushing.

"She's a born grouch," asserted Jerry. "She's been one ever since I've known her. Even in grammar school she was like that. She's always had a fixed idea that because she's poor everyone looks down on her. It's too bad. She's very bright in her studies, and she'd be quite pretty if she didn't go around all the time looking ready to bite."

"Isn't it funny?" mused Marjorie. "I've never noticed her particularly or thought much about her until she made the team as a sub. Since then I've tried several times to talk to her. Each time she has acted as though she didn't like to have me speak to her. I thought maybe she might be a friend of Mignon's. But I suppose it's just because she feels so ashamed of being poor. As if that mattered. We ought to try to make her think differently. She must be terribly unhappy."

"I doubt it," contradicted Jerry. "Some people enjoy being miserable. Probably she's one of that sort. As I said before, 'it's too bad.' Still, one doesn't care to get down on one's knees to somebody, just because that somebody hates herself. She can't expect people are going to like her if she keeps them a mile away from her."

"You are both right," commented Constance. "She ought to be made to understand that being poor isn't a crime. But you can't force that into her head. The only way to do is to wait until a chance comes to prove it to her. We must watch for the psychological moment." Her droll utterance of the last words set her listeners to giggling. Miss Merton was prone to dwell upon that same marvelous psychological moment.

That evening, as Marjorie diligently studied her lessons, the queer, green-eyed little junior again invaded her thoughts. A vision rose of her thin, white face with its pointed chin, sensitive, close-lipped mouth, and wide eyes of bluish-green that frequently changed to a decided green. What a curious, secretive face she had. Marjorie wondered how she had happened to pass by so lightly such a baffling personality. She charitably determined to make up for it by learning to know the true Lucy Warner. She upbraided herself severely for having been so selfish. Absorbed in her own friends, she had neglected to think of how much there was to be done to make the outsiders happy.

Entering the study hall on Monday morning she cast a swift glance toward Lucy's desk. She was rather surprised to note that the blue-green eyes had come to rest on her at the same instant. Marjorie smiled and nodded pleasantly. The other girl only continued to stare fixedly at her, but made no answering sign. Forewarned, Marjorie was not specially concerned over this plain snub. She merely smiled to herself and decided that the psychological moment had evidently not yet arrived.

Slipping into her seat she was about to slide her books into place on the shelf under her desk, when one hand came into contact with something that made her color rise. She drew a sharp breath as she brought it to light. So the Observer was at work again! With a sudden, swift movement of her arm she shoved her find back to cover. Casting a startled look about the study hall, she wondered if whoever had placed it there were now watching her. Strangely enough, the only pair of eyes she caught fastened upon her belonged to Mignon La Salle. In them was a light of brooding scorn, which plainly expressed her opinion of Marjorie.

"Could Mignon be the mysterious Observer?" was again the question that assailed Marjorie's mind. She longed to read the letter, but her pride whispered, "not now." She would save it until school was over for the day. She and Captain would read it together in the living room.

It was a long, weary day for the impatient little girl. At noon she carried the dread missive home with her, gravely intrusting it to her Captain's keeping. "It's another stab from the Observer," she explained soberly. "I haven't opened it. We will read it together when I come home this afternoon. I don't care to read it now."

She returned home that afternoon to find her mother entertaining callers. Despite her feverish impatience to have the thing over, she was her usual charming self to her mother's friends. Nevertheless, she sighed with relief when she saw them depart. Seating herself on the davenport she leaned wearily against its cushioned back. The suspense of not knowing had told severely upon her.

"Now, Lieutenant, I think we are ready," said Mrs. Dean cheerily. Taking the letter from a drawer of the library table, she sat down beside Marjorie and tore open the envelope. Her head against her Captain's shoulder, Marjorie's eyes followed the Observer's latest triumph in letter writing:

"Miss Dean:

"Last Saturday showed very plainly that you could not play basket ball. I knew this long ago. Several others must now know it. It would serve you right if you were asked to resign from the team. If you had been thinking less about yourself and more about the game, you might have tied the score and not disgraced the juniors. You are a menace to the team and ought to be removed from it. As I am not alone in this opinion, I imagine and sincerely hope that you will soon receive your dismissal. If you had any honor in you, you would resign without waiting to be asked. But remember that a coward is soon worsted in the fight. Prepare to meet the inevitable.

"The Observer."

Without speaking, Marjorie turned again to the first page of the letter, re-reading thoughtfully the entire communication. "This letter tells me something which the others didn't," she said.

"It tells me that it is high time to stop such nonsense." Mrs. Dean's tones conveyed righteous indignation. "The whole thing is simply outrageous."

"It can't be stopped until we know who is writing these letters," reminded Marjorie. "But I think I have a tiny clue. That sentence about disgracing the juniors would make it seem that a junior wrote them. No one would mention it who wasn't a junior. I've tried not to believe it, but now I am almost certain that Mignon wrote them. She would like more than anyone else to see me lose my place on the team. Yes, Mignon and the Observer must be very closely related."

CHAPTER XVII—IN TIME OF NEED

Three days later Marjorie's theory seemed destined to prove itself correct. Ellen Seymour came to her, wrath in her eye. "See here, Marjorie," she burst forth impulsively, "if Miss Davis sends for you to meet her in the gym after school, let me know. I'm going there with you. Yesterday while you girls were at practice she stood there watching you. Do you remember?"

"Yes. I noticed her. She stared at me so hard she made me nervous and I played badly. She has always had that effect on me. Last year when she managed the team she was fond of watching me. She used to criticize my playing, too, and call out one thing to me just when I knew I ought to do another. She was awfully fussy. I hope she isn't going to begin it again this year. I thought she had left everything to you."

"So did I," retorted Ellen grimly. "It seems she hasn't. Someone, you can guess who, went to her after the game and said something about your playing. She came to me and said: 'I understand there is a great deal of dissatisfaction on the part of the juniors over Miss Dean's being on the junior team.' You can imagine what I said. When I saw her in the gym after school I knew she had an object. But leave things to me. I know a way to stop her objections very quickly. If she sends for you, go straight to the junior locker room from the study hall and wait there for me. If she doesn't send for you, then you'll know everything is all right. Remember now, don't set foot out of that locker room until I come for you." With this parting injunction Ellen hurried off, leaving Marjorie a victim to many emotions.

So the Observer's, or rather Mignon's, prophesy bordered on fulfillment. Mignon and the few juniors who still adhered to the La Salle standard had made complaint against her to Miss Davis in the name of the junior class. As a friend of Miss Merton, Miss Davis had always favored the French girl. Last year it had been whispered about that her motive in creating a second sophomore team had arisen from her wish to help Mignon's fortunes along. No doubt she had been very glad to listen to this latest appeal on Mignon's part.

But Marjorie was only partially correct in her conclusions. Though it was, indeed, true that Mignon had besieged Miss Davis with a plea that Marjorie be removed from the team, no other member of the junior class had accompanied her. She was flanked by the far more powerful allies, Charlotte Horner and Rowena Farnham. The plan of attack had originated in Rowena's fertile brain as the result of a bitter outburst against Marjorie on Mignon's part. It was directly after the game that she had stormed out her grievances to Rowena and Charlotte. Personally, Rowena cared little about

Mignon's woes. Her mischief-making faculties were aroused merely on Marjorie's account. Had it been Susan, or Muriel against whom Mignon raved she would have laughed and dubbed her friend, "a big baby." But Marjorie—there was a chance to even her score.

"You just let me manage this," Rowena had declared boastfully. "This Miss Davis is easy. She's a snob. So is Miss Merton. If they weren't they'd have put you in your place long ago. They can see through you. It's money that counts with both of them. I've made it a point right along to be nice to Miss Davis. In case that frosty Miss Seymour tried to make trouble for me, I knew I needed a substantial backing. Now I'll ask her to my house to dinner to-morrow night. If she can't come, so much the better for me. If she can, so much the better for you. Of course you'll be there, too. Then we'll see what we can do. You ought to be very grateful to me. I expect she'll bore me to death. I'm only doing it for your sake."

Rowena was too crafty not to hang the heavy mantle of obligation on Mignon's shoulders. Thus indebted to her, Mignon would one day be reminded of the debt. As a last perfect touch to her scheme she had shrewdly included Charlotte Horner in the invitation. Providentially for Mignon, Miss Davis had no previous engagement. So it fell about that Rowena became hostess to three guests. At home a young despot, who bullied her timid little mother and coaxed her indulgent father into doing her will, she merely announced her intention to entertain at dinner and let that end it. The final results of that highly successful dinner party were yet to be announced.

Unwittingly, however, Miss Davis had blundered. In order to strengthen her case she had purposely complained of Marjorie to Ellen Seymour. Knowing nothing of Ellen's devotion to the pretty junior, she had not dreamed that Ellen would set the wheels in motion to defeat her. She was in reality more to be pitied than blamed. Of a nature which accepted hearsay evidence, declining to go below the surface, it is not to be wondered at that Rowena's clever persuasion, backed by Mignon's and Charlotte's able support, caused her to spring to the French girl's aid. She was one of those aggravating persons who refuse to see whatever they do not wish to see. She was undoubtedly proficient in the business of physical culture. She was extremely inefficient in the art of reading girls. Sufficient unto herself, she, therefore, felt no compunction in sending forth the word that should summon Marjorie to the gymnasium, there to be deprived of that which she had rightfully earned.

Like many other days that had come to poor Marjorie since the beginning of her junior year, suspense became the ruling power. Two things she knew definitely. Ellen Seymour was for her. Miss Davis against her. The rest she could only guess at, losing herself in a maze of troubled conjecture. Judge her surprise when on reaching the locker room, she found not only Ellen awaiting her, but her teammates as well. They had made a most precipitate flight from the study hall in order to be in the locker room when she arrived.

"Why, Ellen! Why, girls!" she stammered. A deeper pink rushed to her cheeks; a mist gathered in her eyes as she realized the meaning of their presence. They had come in a body to help her.

"We're here because we're here," trilled Captain Muriel Harding. "In a few minutes we'll be in the gym. Then someone else will get a surprise. Are we ready to march? I rather think we are. Lead the procession, Ellen."

"Come on, Marjorie, you and I will walk together. Fall in, girls. The invincible sextette will now take the trail."

Amid much laughter on their part and openly curious glances from constantly arriving juniors who wondered what was on foot, the six girls had swung off down the corridor before the curious ones found opportunity to relieve their curiosity.

"She's not here yet," commented Susan, as they entered the place of tryst. "Isn't that too bad. I hoped she'd be on hand to see the mighty host advancing."

"Here she comes," warned Rita Talbot. "Now, for it."

CHAPTER XVIII—DOING BATTLE FOR MARJORIE

Two spots of angry color appeared high up on Miss Davis's lean face as she viewed the waiting six. It came to her that she was in for a lively scene. Setting her mouth firmly, she approached them. Addressing herself to Marjorie, she opened with: "I sent for you, Miss Dean; not your friends."

"I asked these girls to come here." Ellen Seymour turned an unflinching gaze upon the nettled instructor.

"Then you may invite them into one of the dressing rooms for a time. My business with Miss Dean is strictly personal."

"I am quite willing that my friends should hear whatever you have to say to me." Marjorie's brown head lifted itself a trifle higher.

"But I am not willing that they should listen," snapped Miss Davis.

"Then I must refuse to listen, also," flashed the quick, but even response.

"This is sheer impudence!" exclaimed Miss Davis. "I sent for you and I insist that you must stay until I give you permission to go. As for these girls——"

"These girls will remain here until Marjorie goes," put in Ellen, admirably self-controlled. "Everyone of them knows already why you wish to see Marjorie Dean. She knows, too. We have come to defend her. I, for one, say that she shall not be dismissed from the team. Her teammates say the same. It is unfair."

"Have I said that she was to be dismissed from the team?" demanded Miss Davis, too much irritated to assert her position as teacher. Ellen's blunt accusation had robbed her of her usual show of dignity.

"Can you say that such was not your intention?" cross-questioned Ellen mercilessly.

Miss Davis could not. She looked the picture of angry guilt. "I shall not answer such an impertinent question," she fumed. "You are all dismissed." Privately, she determined to send for Marjorie the next day during school hours.

"Very well." Ellen bowed her acceptance of the dismissal. "Shall we consider the matter settled?"

"Certainly not." The words leaped sharply to the woman's lips. Realizing she had blundered, she hastily amended. "There is no matter under consideration between you and me."

"Whatever concerns Marjorie's basket ball interests, concerns me. If you send for her again she will not come to you unless we come with her. Am I not right?" She appealed for information to the subject of the discussion.

"You are," was the steady reply.

"This is simply outrageous." Miss Davis completely lost composure. "Do you realize all of you that you are absolutely defying your teacher? Miss Dean deserves to be disciplined. After such a display of discourtesy I refuse to allow her the privilege of playing on the junior basket ball team." Miss Davis continued to express herself, unmindful of the fact that Muriel Harding had slipped away from the group and out of the nearest door. Her temper aroused she held forth at length, ending with: "This disgraceful exhibition of favoritism on your part, Miss Seymour, shows very plainly that you are not fitted to manage basket ball in this school. I shall replace you as manager to-morrow. You, Miss Dean, are dismissed from the junior team. I shall report every one of you to Miss Archer as soon as I leave the gymnasium."

"I believe she is on her way here now," remarked Ellen with satirical impersonality. "Muriel went to find her and ask her to come."

"What!" Miss Davis betrayed small pleasure at this news. Quickly recovering herself she ordered: "You may go at once."

"Here she is." Ellen nodded toward a doorway through which the principal had just entered, Muriel only a step behind her. The senior manager's eyes twinkled satisfaction.

"What seems to be the trouble here, Miss Davis?" The principal came pithily to the point.

"I have been insulted by these disrespectful girls." Miss Davis waved a hand toward the defending sextette.

"That is news I do not relish hearing about my girls. I wish every teacher in this school to be treated with respect. Kindly tell me what reason they gave for doing so."

"I sent for Miss Dean on a personal matter. She insisted on bringing these girls with her. I requested them to leave me alone with Miss Dean. They refused to do so. I dismissed them all, intending to put off my interview with

Miss Dean until to-morrow. Miss Seymour took it upon herself to tell me that Miss Dean would not come to me to-morrow unless accompanied by herself and these girls. Miss Dean declared the same thing. Such conduct is unendurable."

"These young women must have strong reason for such peculiar conduct, or else they have overstepped all bounds," decided Miss Archer impassively. "What have you to say for yourself, Ellen? As a member of the senior class I shall expect a concise explanation."

"We have a very strong reason for our misbehavior." Ellen put a questioning inflection on the last word. "Briefly explained, it is this. Miss Davis has been influenced by certain persons to dismiss Marjorie Dean from the junior basket ball team. Because the juniors lost the game the other day by two points, the blame for it has been unjustly placed upon Marjorie. At practice yesterday she did not play as well as usual. These are, apparently, the very shaky causes for her dismissal. I shall not attempt to tell you the true reasons. They are unworthy of mention. As her manager I refused to countenance such unfairness. So did her teammates. They will agree with me when I say that Marjorie is one of the best players we have ever had at Sanford High. We are all in position to say so. We know her work. So we came with her to defend her. I admit that we took a rather stiff stand with Miss Davis. There was no other way."

"What are your reasons for dismissing Miss Dean from the team?" Still impassive of feature, the principal now addressed Miss Davis.

"I have received complaints regarding her work," came the defiant answer.

"According to Ellen these complaints did not proceed from either herself or her teammates. If not from them, whom could it interest to make complaint?" continued the inexorable questioner.

"The members of the junior class are naturally interested in the team representing them," reminded Miss Davis tartly.

"How many members of the junior class objected to Miss Dean as a player?" relentlessly pursued Miss Archer.

Miss Davis grew confused. "I—they—I decline to talk this matter over with you in the presence of these insolent girls," she hotly rallied.

"A word, girls, and you may go. I am greatly displeased over this affair. Since basket ball seems to be such a trouble-breeder, it might better be abolished in this school. I may decide to take that step. Desperate diseases require desperate remedies. You will hear more of this later. That will be all at present."

With the feeling that the gymnasium roof was about to descend upon them, the six girls quitted the battlefield.

"Don't you ever believe Miss Archer will stop basket ball," emphasized Muriel Harding when they were well down the corridor. "She knows every single thing about it. I told her in the office. I told her, too, that I knew Rowena Farnham and Charlotte Horner were mixed up in it. They've had their heads together ever since the game."

"I would have resigned in a minute, but I just couldn't after the way you girls fought for me," Marjorie voiced her distress. "If Miss Archer stops basket ball it will be my fault. I'm sorry I ever made the team."

"You couldn't help yourself." Ellen Seymour was rapidly regaining her cheerfulness. "Don't think for a minute that Miss Davis will be able to smooth things over. Miss Archer is too clever not to recognize unfairness when she meets it face to face. And don't worry about her stopping basket ball. Take my word for it. She won't."

CHAPTER XIX—WHAT JERRY MACY "DUG UP"

As Ellen Seymour had predicted, basket ball did not receive its quietus. But no one ever knew what passed between Miss Archer and Miss Davis. The principal also held a long session with Ellen, who emerged from her office with a pleased smile. To Marjorie and her faithful support Ellen said confidentially: "It's all settled. No one will ever try to shove Marjorie off the team while Miss Archer is here. But basket ball is doomed, if anything else like that ever comes up. Miss Archer says so." Strangely enough the six girls were not required to apologize to Miss Davis. Possibly Miss Archer was not anxious to reopen the subject by thus courting fresh rebellion. After all, basket ball was not down on the high school curriculum. She was quite willing her girls should be at liberty to manage it as they chose, provided they managed it wisely and without friction. Privately, she was disgusted with Miss Davis's part in the recent disagreement. She strongly advised the former to give up all claim to the management of the teams. But this advice Miss Davis refused to take. She still insisted on keeping up a modified show of authority, but resolved within herself to be more careful. She had learned considerable about girls.

The three plotters accepted their defeat with bad grace. Afraid that the tale would come to light, Mignon and Charlotte privately shoved the blame on Rowena's shoulders. Nothing leaked out, however, and they were too wise to censure Rowena to her face. Mignon soon discovered that the obliging sophomore's efforts in her behalf had cost her dear. Rowena tyrannized over her more than ever. After the second game between the junior and sophomore teams, which occurred two weeks after Marjorie's narrow escape from dismissal from the team, Mignon came into the belief that her lot was, indeed, hard. The sophomores had been ingloriously beaten, the score standing - in favor of the juniors. In consequence Rowena was furious, forcing Mignon to listen to her long tirades against the juniors, and rating her unmercifully when she failed to register proper sympathy.

Owing to the nearness of the Christmas holidays and the brief stretch that lay between them and the mid-year examinations, the other two games were put off until February and March, respectively. No one except Rowena was sorry. She longed for a speedy opportunity to wipe the defeat off her slate. She had little of the love of holiday giving in her heart, and was heard loudly to declare that Christmas was a nuisance.

Marjorie and her little coterie of intimates regarded it very differently. They found the days before Yule-tide altogether too short in which to carry out their Christmas plans. With the nearness of the blessed anniversary of the world's King, Marjorie grew daily happier. Since the straightening of the basket ball tangle, for her, things in school had progressed with surprising smoothness. Then, too, the hateful Observer had evidently forgotten her. Since the letter advising her to "prepare to meet the inevitable," the Observer had apparently laid down her pen. Marjorie soberly confided to her captain that she hoped Christmas might make the Observer see things differently.

Obeying the familiar mandate, which peered at her from newspaper, store or street car, "Do Your Christmas Shopping Early," she lovingly stored away the numerous beribboned bundles designed for intimate friends at least a week before Christmas. That last week she left open in order to go about the business of making a merry Christmas for the needy. As on the previous year Jerry Macy and Constance were her right-hand men. Susan, Irma, Muriel and Harriet also caught the fever of giving and the six girls worked zealously, inspired by the highest motives, to bring happiness to the poverty-stricken.

Christmas morning brought Marjorie an unusual windfall of gifts. It seemed as though everyone she liked had remembered her. Looking back on the previous Christmas, she remembered rather sadly the Flag of Truce and all that it had signified. This year Mary and she were again one at heart. She dropped a few tears of sheer happiness over Mary's long Christmas letter and the beautiful embroidered Mexican scarf that had come with it. She had sent Mary a wonderful silver desk set engraved with M. to M., which she hoped wistfully that Mary would like as much as she cherished her exquisite scarf.

The Christmas vacation was, as usual, a perpetual round of gaiety. Jerry and Hal gave their usual dance. Constance gave a New Year's hop. Harriet and Muriel entertained their friends at luncheons, while Marjorie herself sent out invitations for an old-fashioned sleigh-ride party, with an informal supper and dance at her home on the return. These social events, with some few others of equal pleasure, sent Father Time spinning along giddily.

"Aren't you sorry it's all over?" sighed Constance, as she and Marjorie lingered at the Macys' gate at the close of their first day at school after the holidays.

"Sorry's no name for it," declared Jerry. "We certainly had one beautiful time, I mean a beautiful time. Honestly, I liked the getting things ready for other folks best of all, though. I like to keep busy. I wish we had something to do or somebody to help all the time. I'm going to poke around and see what I can stir up. I try to do the sisterly, helpful act toward Hal; picking up the stuff he strews all over the house and locating lost junk, I mean articles, but he's about as appreciative as a Feejee Islander. You know how grateful they are."

"I saw one in a circus once," laughed Constance reminiscently. "I wasn't impressed with his sense of gratitude. Someone threw him a peanut and he flung it back and hit an old gentleman in the eye."

A general giggle arose at the erring Feejee's strange conception of gratitude.

"That will be nice to tell Hal when he shows the same delicate sort of thankfulness," grinned Jerry. "I'm not going to waste my precious talents on him all winter. I'm going to dig up something better. If you girls hear of anything, run all the way to our house, any hour of the day or night, and tell your friend Jerry Geraldine Jeremiah. All three are one, as Rudyard Kipling says in something or other he wrote."

"I love Kipling's books," said Constance. "One of the first things I did when I wasn't poor any longer was to buy a whole set. That first year at Sanford High I tried to get them in the school library. But there were only two or three of them."

"That library is terribly run down," asserted Jerry. "They haven't half the books there they ought to have. I was talking to my father about it the other night. He promised to put it before the Board. I hope he does. Then maybe we'll get some more books. I don't care so much for myself. I can get all the books I want. But there are a lot of girls that can't, who need special ones for reading courses."

Jerry's resolve to "poke around and stir up something" did not meet with any special success. The more needy of the Christmas poor were already being looked after by Mrs. Dean, Mrs. Macy and other charitably disposed persons who devoted themselves to the cause of benevolence the year around. Generous-hearted Jerry continued to help in the good work, but her active nature was still on the alert for some special object.

"I've dug it up," she announced in triumph, several evenings later. The three girls were conducting a prudent review at Jerry's home, preparatory to the rapidly approaching mid-year test.

"What did you say, Jerry?" Marjorie tore her eyes from her French grammar, over which she had been poring. "I was so busy trying to fix the conjugation of these miserable, irregular verbs in my mind that I didn't hear you."

"I've dug up the great idea; the how-to-be-helpful stunt. It's right in our school, too, that our labors are needed."

"That's interesting; ever so much more so than this." Constance Stevens closed the book she held with a snap. "I'm not a bit fond of German," she added. "I have to study it, though, on account of the Wagner operas. This 'Höher als die Kirche' is a pretty story, but it's terribly hard to translate. We'll have several pages of it to do in examination. Excuse me, Jerry, for getting off the subject. What is it that you've dug up?"

"It's about the library. You know I told you that my father was going to speak of it at the Board meeting. Well, he did, but it wasn't any use. There have been such a lot of appropriations made for other things that the library will have to wait. That's what the high and mighty Board say. This is what I say. Why not get busy among ourselves and dig up some money for new books?"

"You mean by subscription?" asked Marjorie.

"No, siree. I mean by earning it ourselves," proposed Jerry. "Subscription would mean that a lot of girls would feel that they ought to give something which they couldn't afford to give. Then there'd be those who couldn't give a cent. That would be hard on them. What we ought to do is to get up some kind of a show that the whole school would be interested in."

"That's a fine idea. It's public-spirited," approved Marjorie. "What sort of entertainment do you think we might give? We couldn't give it until after examinations, though."

"I know the kind I'd like to give, but I can't unless a certain person promises to help me," was Jerry's mystifying reply.

"Miss Archer?" guessed Constance.

"Nope; Connie Stevens." Jerry grinned widely at Constance's patent amazement.

"I?" she questioned. "What have I to do with it?"

"Everything. You could coax Laurie Armitage to help us and then, too, you'd be leading lady. Do you know now what I'm driving at? I see you don't. Well, I'd like to give the 'Rebellious Princess' again, one night in Sanford and the next in Riverview. That is only twenty-five miles from here. A whole lot of the Sanfordites were disappointed last year because they couldn't get into the theatre to see the operetta. Another performance would pack the theatre, just as full as last Spring. I know the Riverview folks would turn out to it. There are two high schools in Riverview, you know. Besides, we have the costumes and everything ready. Two or three rehearsals would be all we'd need. If we tried to give an entertainment or a play, it would take so long to practise for it. Have I a head on my shoulders or have I not?"

"You certainly have," chorused her listeners.

"I am willing to do all I can," agreed Constance. "I'll see Laurie about it to-morrow."

"Oh, you needn't wait until then. He's downstairs now with Hal and Danny Seabrooke. I told Hal to ask the boys over here this evening. We can't study all the time, you know. I suppose they are ready to tear up the furniture because we are still up here. Danny Seabrooke is such a sweet, patient, little boy. Put away your books and we'll go down to the library. Since this is a library proposition, let's be consistent."

A hum of girl voices, accompanied by the patter of light feet on the stairs, informed three impatient youths that they had not waited in vain.

"At last!" exclaimed the irrepressible Daniel, better known as the Gad-fly, his round, freckled face almost disappearing behind his Cheshire grin. "Long have we sought thee, and now that we have found thee——"

"Sought nothing," contradicted Jerry. "I'll bet you haven't set foot outside this library. There's evidence of it." She pointed to Hal and Laurie, who had just hastily deposited foils in a corner and were now more hastily engaged in drawing on their coats. "You've been holding a fencing match. Laurie came out best, of course. He always does. He's a fencing master and a musician all in one."

"Jerry never gives me credit for anything," laughed Hal. "That is, in public. Later, when Laurie's gone home, she'll tell me how much better I can fence than Laurie."

"Don't you believe him. He's trying to tease me, but I know him too well to pay any attention to what he says." Jerry's fond grin bespoke her affection for the brother she invariably grumbled about. At heart she was devoted to him. In public she derived peculiar pleasure from sparring with him.

The trio of girls had advanced upon the library, there to hold a business session. But the keynote of the next half hour was sociability. It was Constance who first started the ball rolling. Ensconced beside Laurie on the deep window seat, she told the young composer that Jerry had a wonderful scheme to unfold.

"Then let's get together and listen to it," he said warmly. Three minutes afterward he had marshalled the others to the window seat. "Everybody sit down but Jerry. She has the floor. Go ahead, Jerry. Tell us what you'd like us to do." He reseated himself by Constance. Laurie never neglected an opportunity to be near to the girl of his boyish heart.

Posting herself before her hearers with an exaggerated air of importance, Jerry made a derisive mouth at Danny Seabrooke, who was leaning forward with an appearance of profound interest, which threatened to land him sprawling on the floor. "I'm not used to addressing such a large audience," she chuckled. "Ahem! Wow!" Having delivered herself of these enlightening remarks she straightened her face and set forth her plan with her usual brusque energy. She ended with: "You three boys have got to help. No backing out."

"Surely we'll help," promised Laurie at once. "It's a good idea, Jerry. I can have things going inside of a week. That is, if my leading lady doesn't develop a temperament. These opera singers are very temperamental, you know." His blue eyes rested smilingly on Constance.

"I'm not an opera singer," she retorted. "I'm only a would-be one. Would-be's are very humble persons. They know they must behave well. You had better interview your tenor lead. Tenors are supposed to be terribly irresponsible."

Amid an exchange of equally harmless badinage, the six willing workers discussed the plan at length. So much excited discussion was provocative of hunger. No one, except Hal, said so, yet when Jerry disappeared to return trundling a tea wagon, filled with delectable provender, she was hailed with acclamation.

"What splendid times we always have together," was Marjorie's enthusiastic opinion, when seated beside Hal in his own pet car she was being conveyed home. Snatches of mirthful conversation issuing from the tonneau where the rest of the sextette, Jerry included, were enjoying themselves hugely, seemed direct corroboration of her words. Invited to "come along," Jerry had needed no second urging.

"That's your fault," Hal made gallant response. "You are the magnet that draws us all together. Before you and Jerry were friends I never realized what a fine sister I had. If you hadn't been so nice to Constance, she and Laurie might never have come to know each other so well. Then there's Dan. He always used to run away from girls. He got over his first fright at that little party you gave the first year you came to Sanford. You're a magician, Marjorie, and you're making a pretty nice history for yourself among your friends. I hope always to be among the best of them." Hal was very earnest in his boyish praise.

"I am sure we'll always be the best of friends, Hal," she said seriously, though her color heightened at the sincere tribute to herself. "I can't see that I've done anything specially wonderful, though. It's easy to be nice to those one likes who like one in return. It's being nice to those one doesn't like that's hard. It's harder still not to be liked."

"Then you aren't apt to know that hardship," retorted Hal.

Marjorie smiled faintly. She had known that very hardship ever since she had come to Sanford. She merely answered: "Everybody must meet a few, I won't say enemies, I'll just say, people who don't like one."

That night as she sat before her dressing table brushing her thick, brown curls, she pondered thoughtfully over Hal Macy's words. In saying them she knew he had been sincere. It was sweet to hope that she had been and was still a power for good. Yet it made her feel very humble. She could only resolve to try always to live up to that difficult standard.

CHAPTER XX—CONSTANCE POINTS THE WAY

"This is a nice state of affairs," scolded Jerry Macy. "What do you suppose has happened, Marjorie?" Overtaking her friend in the corridor on the way from recitation, Jerry's loud question cut the air like a verbal bomb-shell. Without waiting for a reply she continued in a slightly lower key. "Harriet has tonsilitis. Isn't that the worst you ever heard? And only three days before the operetta, too. We can't give it until she gets well, unless somebody in the chorus can sing her rôle. I'm going to telephone Laurie after my next class is over and tell him about it. The chorus is our only hope. Some one of the girls may know the part fairly well. They all ought to after so much rehearsing last Spring. Most of them can't do solo work, though. Do you think you could sing it?" Jerry had drawn Marjorie to one side of the corridor as she rapidly related her bad news.

"Mercy, no!" Marjorie registered dismay at the mere suggestion. "I wouldn't dream of attempting it. Isn't it too bad that Harriet hasn't an understudy? I'm ever so sorry she's sick. How dreadfully disappointed she must be."

"Not any more so than half of Sanford will be when they hear the operetta's been postponed. Every reserved seat ticket's been sold. Who'd have thought that Harriet would go and get tonsilitis?" mourned Jerry. "There's a regular epidemic of it in Sanford. You know Nellie Simmons had it when the sophs wanted that basket ball game postponed. Quite a number of Sanford High girls have had it, too. Be careful you don't get it."

Marjorie laughed. "Oh, I won't. Don't worry. I'm never sick. We'll have to go, Jerry. There's the last bell."

"You had better touch wood." Jerry hurled this warning advice over one plump shoulder as she moved off.

It brought a smile to Marjorie's lips. She was not in the least superstitious. She grew grave with the thought that the operetta would have to be postponed. At the first performance of the "Rebellious Princess," Harriet had sung her part at a moment's notice. Until then she had been Mignon La Salle's understudy. Struck by a sudden thought Marjorie stopped short. Jerry had evidently forgotten that Mignon knew the rôle. Still, it would do no good to remind her of it, or Laurie either. She believed that Jerry, at least, would infinitely prefer that the operetta should never be given rather than allow Mignon to sing in it. The mere mention of it was likely to make her cross. Marjorie decided to keep her own counsel. She had no reason to wish to see Mignon thus honored, particularly after her treacherous attempt to do

Constance out of her part. Then, too, there was the new grievance of the Observer against her.

By the time school was over for the day, Constance had already been acquainted with the dire news. Apart from her two chums, Jerry had told no one else except Hal and Laurie. When the three girls emerged from the school building, accompanied by Susan, Muriel and Irma, they saw the two young men waiting for them across the street. The latter three faithful satellites immediately took themselves off with much giggling advice to Jerry that four was a company, but five a crowd. Jerry merely grinned amiably and refused to join them. She knew her own business.

"This is too bad, Jerry," were Laurie's first words. "What are we to do?"

"That's for you to say," shrugged Jerry. "All I can think of to do is have a try-out of the chorus. If none of them can sing Harriet's part, we'll have to call it off. I mean postpone it." Jerry cast a sly glance at Hal to see if he had noticed her polite amendment.

"What have you to say, Constance and Marjorie?" queried Laurie. "But the street is not the place for a consultation. Suppose we go down to Sargent's to talk it over. I spoke to Professor Harmon this afternoon, but he said he'd rather leave it to me. He's busy just now with that new boy choir at the Episcopal Church. He wants me to direct the operetta."

Voicing approval of this last, the three girls allowed their willing cavaliers to steer them toward Sargent's hospitable doors. Hal, Marjorie and Jerry took the lead, leaving Constance and Laurie to follow. Nothing further relating to the problem that had risen was said until the five were seated at a rear table in the confectioner's smart little shop. Then Laurie abruptly took it up. "We are ready for suggestions," he invited.

"I have one." There was a peculiar note of uncertainty in Constance's voice as she spoke. "You are not going to be pleased with it, but it seems to me the only thing to do." More boldly she added: "Let Mignon La Salle sing the part."

"Never!" burst from Laurie and Jerry simultaneously.

The appearance of a white-coated youth to take their order halted the discussion for a moment. As he hurried away Marjorie's soft voice was heard: "I thought of that, too, this morning. I had made up my mind not to speak of it. Connie makes me ashamed of myself. Connie is willing for Mignon to sing the part that she cheated herself of. I think we ought to be."

In silence Laurie stared at her across the table, his brows knitted in a deep frown. Then his gaze rested on Constance. "You girls are queer," he said slowly. "I don't understand you at all."

"I do," declared Jerry, far from pleased. "I can't say I agree with them, though. If we ask Mignon to sing the part (I don't know who's going to ask her), she will parade around like a peacock. She may say 'no' just for spite. She doesn't speak to any of us." Then she added in a milder tone, "I suppose her father would dance a hornpipe if we let her sing it. I heard he felt terribly about the way she performed last Spring. You know he put off a business trip just to go to hear her sing, and then she didn't. She had nobody but herself to blame, though."

Unwittingly, Jerry had struck a responsive chord in Hal. Leaning forward, he said impulsively, "Then I think I'd ask her, Laurie. Mr. La Salle is a fine man. His office is next to Dad's. I often go in there and talk to him. He is mighty interesting. He has traveled all over the world and knows how to tell about what he's seen. He's all wrapped up in Mignon. You can see that. I wish you'd ask her just on his account. It would pay up for last Spring."

"Three against two," grumbled Jerry, "and one of them my own brother. Do we stand our ground, Laurie, or do we not?"

Laurie did not answer immediately. He had not forgiven the French girl her transgression against Constance. The battery of earnest blue and brown eyes bent upon him proved fatal to his animosity. "Our ground seems to be shaky," he answered. "The majority generally rules."

"Then you will ask her?" Constance flashed him a radiant smile that quite repaid him for his hinted decision in Mignon's favor. "It will have to be you. She wouldn't do it for us."

Laurie showed lively consternation. "Oh, see here——" Innate chivalry toward girlhood overtook him. "All right," he answered. "I'll ask her."

In the midst of countless woes, arising from her unwilling allegiance to Rowena Farnham, Mignon next day received the glorious invitation from a most studiedly polite young man. If anyone other than Lawrence Armitage had come to her with the request she would, in all probability, refused pointblank to countenance the idea. Mignon still cherished her school-girl preference for the handsome young musician. She, therefore, assented to the proposal with only the merest show of reluctance. Laurie made it very plain, however, that Constance Stevens desired it. Inwardly, Mignon writhed with anger; outwardly, she was a smiling image of amiability.

Afterward she experienced the deepest satisfaction in boasting to Rowena of the honor which had come to her.

"I think I'll be in that operetta, too," had been Rowena's calm decision. "I'll go to that Lawrence Armitage and tell him I shall sing in the chorus." Straightway, she went on this laudable errand, only to be politely but firmly informed that there were no chorus vacancies. Over this she raged to Mignon, then consoled herself and dismayed the French girl by calmly announcing, "I'm going to the theatre with you just the same and watch the silly operetta from behind the scenes. Let me know when you have your rehearsals, for I intend to go to them, too."

Resorting to craft, Mignon managed to attend the first rehearsal without Rowena. The latter discovered this and pounced upon her on her way home with a torrent of ungentle remarks. Bullied to tears, Mignon was obliged to allow Rowena to accompany her to the second and third rehearsals, the third being the last before the public performance.

Though the cast secretly objected to this, they made no open manifestation of their disgust. It was now fairly well known how matters stood between Rowena and Mignon. The latter had no reason to complain of the universally civil treatment she received. It was merely civil, however, and contained no friendliness of spirit. By the entire cast the French girl was regarded as an evil necessity. For that reason they also reluctantly endured Rowena's presence. But Rowena derived no pleasure from her intrusion, except the fact that she was a source of covert annoyance to all parties. Her jealous soul was filled with torment at being left out of the production. Shrewd intuition alone warned her not to create even the slightest disturbance. She had determined to go with the cast to Riverview. Consequently, she did not propose cutting off her nose to spite her face.

The knowledge that the proceeds from the operetta were to be devoted to school use, rallied the Sanfordites to the cause. The Sanford performances went off without a hitch before a huge and delighted assemblage. It may be set down to her credit that Mignon La Salle sang the part of the proud stepsister even better than Harriet Delaney had rendered it. Her dramatic ability was considerable and her voice and temperament were eminently suited to her rôle. On this one occasion her long-suffering parent was not disappointed in his daughter. Natural perspicacity caused him to wonder not a little how it had all come about, and he made a mental note to inquire into it at the first opportunity. Strongly disapproving of the intimacy between Mignon and Rowena Farnham, he was hopeful that this honor done his daughter would throw her again among the finer type of the Sanford girls. From his young friend Hal Macy he had received glowing descriptions of Marjorie and her close friends, and he longed to see Mignon take kindly to them.

Could he have peeped into Mignon's subtle brain, his dreams would have vanished in thin air. Ever the ingrate, she was thankful to none for the unexpected chance to glitter. At heart she was the same tigerish young person, ready to claw at a moment's notice. Within her lurked two permanent desires. One of them was to win the interest of Lawrence Armitage; the other to be free of Rowena.

CHAPTER XXI—ROWENA RE-ARRANGES MATTERS

The Sanford performance of "The Rebellious Princess" took place on Friday evening. Late the following afternoon the illustrious cast were conveyed by train or motor to Riverview, the scene of Saturday evening's operations. Marjorie, Constance, Mr. and Mrs. Dean drove there in the Deans' motor. Accompanied by Mrs. Macy, Jerry, Susan, Muriel and Irma motored to Riverview together. Hal and Laurie sought temporary freedom from the fair sex in the latter's roadster. Mr. La Salle had promised, at Mignon's earnest request, to drive to Riverview with her in her runabout. She had adopted this means of thus temporarily eliminating Rowena. Not daring to thrust herself upon Mignon when bolstered by her father's protection, Rowena had declared buoyantly that she would be there anyway.

Unfortunately for Mignon, a sudden business emergency sent Mr. La Salle speeding to Buffalo on the Saturday morning train. Before going, however, he instructed his chauffeur to drive Mignon to the train for Riverview and see her safely on it. With others of the cast on the same train, she would be in good company. But the best laid plans often go astray. Ever on the alert for treachery, Rowena saw Mr. La Salle depart and hurrying to the La Salle's home soon bullied the true state of affairs from his petulant offspring.

"Don't bother about taking the train," Rowena counseled arrogantly. "James will drive us over to Riverview in our limousine. He can stay there until the show is over and bring us home."

"I can't do that," parried Mignon. "My father gave orders to William to drive me to the train the cast is to take and put me on it. If I were to go with you, William would tell him."

"Oh, no, he wouldn't," retorted Rowena. "Just let me talk to William." Without waiting for further excuses from Mignon, the self-willed sophomore dashed out of the house in the direction of the La Salle garage. Mignon followed her, divided between vexation and approbation. She was far from anxious to make the journey to Riverview by train. For once Rowena stood for the lesser of two evils.

"Come here, William," called Rowena, pausing outside the open garage door and imperiously beckoning the chauffeur who was engaged in putting a fresh tire on Mignon's runabout.

"What is it, Miss?" asked the man, as he frowningly approached Rowena.

"You needn't take Miss La Salle to the train this afternoon. She's going with me. She has so much luggage she can't manage it on the train, so she had to make different arrangements." Rowena presented a formidably smiling front as she gave her command.

"But Mr. La Salle——" protested William.

"Don't be impertinent," was the freezing interruption. "We know our own business. Miss La Salle's father will know all about it when he returns. Won't he?" She turned to Mignon for confirmation.

"It is all right, William," the latter assured him, purposely neglecting to answer Rowena's question. "My father will be told when he returns. He forgot about my luggage."

"All right, Miss Mignon." William was far too discreet to court the double attack, which he knew would be forthcoming, should he continue to protest. Miss Mignon always did as she pleased, regardless of her father. He made mental note, however, to clear himself the instant his employer returned.

"That was simple enough," exulted Rowena, as they turned away. "You ought to be glad I fixed everything so nicely for you. I expect some of those snippy girls will be anything but pleased to have me behind the scenes to-night."

"You'd better keep to my dressing room," warned Mignon. "On account of it being a different theatre, there is sure to be some confusion. Laurie Armitage won't like it if you go strolling around among the cast the way you've done at rehearsals."

"You just attend to your own affairs," blustered Rowena, "and I'll attend to mine. Who cares what that high and mighty Lawrence Armitage thinks? He's so wrapped up in that milk-and-water baby of a Constance Stevens he doesn't know you are alive. Too bad, isn't it?"

Mignon turned red as a poppy. She began to wish she had not allowed Rowena to alter the arrangements her father had prudently made. Frowning her displeasure at the brutal taunt, she cast a half-longing glance toward the garage. There was still time to inform William that she had changed her mind.

Instantly Rowena marked the glance and divined its import. It did not accord with her plans. If she drove Mignon to reconsider her decision, it meant one of two things. To quarrel openly with her would place beyond reach the possibility of accompanying her to Riverview. If Rowena went there alone she could not hope to be allowed to go behind the scenes. On the other hand she dared not jeopardize her control over Mignon by permitting her to gain even one point.

"Don't be foolish," she advised in a more conciliatory tone. "I was only teasing you about that Stevens girl. One of these days this Armitage boy will find out what a silly little thing she is. If you are nice to me, I daresay I can help him to find it out."

Mignon brightened visibly. From all she had learned of Rowena's practical methods, she believed her capable of accomplishing wonders in the mischief-making line. "I suppose you mean well," she said a trifle sullenly. "Still, I don't think you ought to say such cutting things to me, Rowena."

Thus once more a temporary truce was declared between these two wayward children of impulse. Though neither trusted the other, sheer love of self admonished them that they could accomplish more by hanging together. Mignon, however, was destined to learn that an unstable prop is no more to be relied upon than no prop at all.

CHAPTER XXII—THE RESULT OF PLAYING WITH FIRE

"See here, Jerry, can't something be done to keep that Miss Farnham from completely upsetting the cast?" Laurie Armitage's fine face was dark with disapproval as he halted Jerry, who was hurrying by him toward Constance's dressing room. "I just heard her telling one of the girls in the chorus that her costume was 'frightfully unbecoming.' The poor girl turned red and looked ready to cry. She's been circulating among the chorus ever since she and Mignon landed in the theatre. Goodness knows what else she has been saying. It won't do. This isn't Sanford, you know. We hope to give a perfect performance here. I wish I had told Mignon not to bring her. I hated to do it, though. She might have got wrathy and backed out at the last minute. If ever I compose another operetta, I'll let somebody else manage it. I'm through," Laurie concluded in disgust.

"Why don't you ask Mignon to keep her in the dressing room?" suggested Jerry. "She's the only one who can manage Row-ena. I doubt if she can."

"Might as well touch a match to a bundle of firecrackers," compared Laurie gloomily. "Can't you think of anything else?"

Jerry studied for a moment. As Laurie's helper she felt that she ought to measure up to the situation. "It's almost time for the show to begin," she said. "The chorus will soon be too busy to bother with her. After the first act, she'll be in Mignon's dressing room. Then I'll slip around among the girls and whisper to them not to mind her. She can't bother the principals. She doesn't dare go near Constance or any of the boys like Hal and the Crane."

"Please do that." Laurie sighed with relief. "It will help me a great deal."

Unaware that she had become the victim of a needful strategy, Rowena was serenely deriving huge enjoyment from the brutally frank criticisms she was lavishing right and left among the unoffending choirsters. It was a supreme happiness to her to see her carefully delivered shots strike home. But her ambition to wound lay not entirely with the chorus. She was yearning for a chance to nettle Constance Stevens, whom she hated by reason of the impassable gulf that lay between Constance and herself. Never, since she had come to Sanford, had Constance appeared even to know that she existed. This galled Rowena beyond expression. As a leader among the high school girls she had deemed Constance worth cultivating. She might as readily have tried to bring down the North Star as to ingratiate herself with this calm, lovely girl, and she knew it. Here was something which she could not obtain. Failing, she marked her as a victim for ridicule and scorn.

The first act over at last, Rowena posted herself in Mignon's dressing room and proceeded to regale the latter with a derisive, laughing account of her fruitful wanderings among the cast. Mignon listened to her with indifference. As she opened the second act, her mind was on her rôle. She was hardly aware that her tormentor had left the dressing room until she became conscious that the high-pitched tones had suddenly ceased.

Mignon proving altogether too non-committal to suit her difficult fancy, Rowena had fared forth in search of fresh adventure. The star dressing room, occupied by Constance, lay two doors farther down the corridor. In passing and repassing it that evening, Rowena had vainly ransacked her guileful brain for an excuse to invade it. Now as she left Mignon's dressing room she decided to put on an intrepid front and pay Constance a call. Her large, black eyes danced with pure malice as she doubled a fist and pounded upon the closed door.

"Who is there?" came from within. The vigorous tattoo had startled Constance.

For answer Rowena simply swung open the door and stepped into the room. "I thought I'd pay you a call," she announced with cool complacence.

Seated before a low make-up shelf on which reposed a mirror, Constance was engaged in readjusting her coiffure, which had become slightly loosened during the first act. Her blue eyes showed wondering surprise as she turned in her chair to face the intruder. From Jerry she had already heard angry protests against this mischievous girl. Quiet Constance now read fresh mischief in the intrusion. She resolved to treat her uninvited guest civilly. If possible she would try to keep her in the dressing room until the second act was called. Better that than allow her to further annoy the other girls. As she had no change of costume to make she was free to entertain her unbidden visitor.

"Sit down," she evenly invited, neither cordial nor cold. "How do you like the operetta?"

Rather taken aback by this placid reception, Rowena dropped gracefully into a chair, her dark eyes fixed speculatively on her hostess. Shrugging her shoulders she gave a contemptuous little laugh as she answered: "Oh, these amateur productions are all alike. Some, of course, are more stupid than others."

"Do you include the poor Princess among the more stupid?" asked Constance, smiling in spite of herself at this patent attempt to be disagreeable.

"I don't include it in anything. I don't even know what it's all about. I only came to rehearsals and here to amuse myself. Sanford is the deadest town I was ever in and Sanford High School is a regular kindergarten. I suppose you know who I am, don't you?" Rowena crested her auburn head a trifle.

"Yes. You are Miss Farnham." Constance made reply in an enigmatic tone.

A threatening sparkle leaped to the other's eyes. She was beginning to resent Constance's quiet attitude. "If you knew who I was, why didn't you speak to me at the first rehearsal?" she sharply launched.

"I merely knew you by sight. There are many girls in Sanford High whom I do not know personally."

"But I'm different," pursued Rowena. "My father is very rich and I can have whatever I like. You must know that. You ought to associate with girls of your own class. Your aunt has lots of money and can give you social position. That Geraldine Macy is the only rich girl you ever go with. All the others are just middle class. You're foolish to waste your time on Marjorie——"

Constance had received Rowena's first words with secret amusement. As she continued to listen her inward smile changed to outward, rather. At mention of Marjorie her self-imposed placidity flew to the winds. "Kindly leave my dressing room," she ordered, her voice shaking with indignation. "Marjorie Dean is my dearest friend. No one can belittle her to me. Least of all, you." Constance had slowly risen, her blue eyes dark with the injury to one she loved.

"I thought that would bring you to life," laughed Rowena, making no move to rise. As she sat there, the light playing on her ruddy hair, her black eyes agleam with tantalizing mirth, Constance could not but wonder at her tigerish beauty. To quote Muriel, she did resemble "a big, striped tiger."

Without answering, Constance moved to the door and opened it. She was about to step into the corridor when Rowena sprang forward and clutched her by the arm. "You milk-and-water baby, do you think——" She did not finish. As Constance stepped over the threshold she came almost into collision with Lawrence Armitage. His keen glance immediately took in the situation. He saw Rowena's arm drop to her side. Brushing past Constance like a whirlwind, she gained the shelter of Mignon's dressing room and disappeared.

"Hurry. You'll miss your cue. I didn't see you in the wings and came to warn you. Run along. I'll see you later," uttered Laurie rapidly. His words sent

Constance moving rapidly toward the stairway. His lips tightened as he watched her disappear. For a moment he stood still, then, turning, took the same direction.

"Just a moment, Miss La Salle." Seeking the stairway at the close of the second act, Mignon was halted by a troubled young man. "I don't wish to be disagreeable, but—Miss Farnham must either remain in your dressing room during the third act or go out in the audience. I am not blaming you. You've sung your part splendidly to-night and I appreciate your effort. Will you help me in this? We don't wish anything to occur to spoil the rest of the operetta. I am sure you understand." Appeal looked out from his deeply blue eyes.

"Of course I'll help you." Mignon experienced a sudden thrill of triumph. Lawrence Armitage was actually asking her to do him a favor. Valiance rose within her. She quite forgot her dread of Rowena's bluster. Flashing him her most fascinating smile, she held out her hand in token of good faith. Inwardly she was hoping that Constance might happen along to witness the tableau. Laurie clasped it lightly. He was not in the least impressed. "Thank you." He wheeled abruptly and turned away.

Mignon ran lightly down the stairs and to her dressing room. Inspired by the recent interview, she promptly accosted the ubiquitous Rowena, as she lounged lazily in a chair. "You mustn't go out of the dressing room or upstairs again until the operetta is over," she dictated. "Laurie doesn't want you to. He just spoke to me about it. He has allowed you a lot of liberty already, so I think you'd better do as he says. It won't be long now until——"

"So Laurie thinks he can order me about, does he?" Rowena sprang to her feet in a rage. "That for Laurie!" She snapped contemptuous fingers. "This is your work. You've been talking about me to him. But you'll be sorry. I know a way——"

Her mood swiftly changing she threw back her head and laughed. Resuming her chair she sat silently eyeing Mignon with a mirthful malevolence that sent a shiver of apprehension up and down the French girl's spine. Rowena had undoubtedly been inspired with an idea that boded no good to her. As she dressed for the third act she cast more than one nervous glance at the smiling figure of insolence in the chair.

Not a word further had been exchanged between the two when the third act was called. Mignon half expected to see Rowena rise and follow her up the stairs, there to create a scene with Laurie that would delay the rise of the curtain. Nothing of the kind occurred, however, and the last act began and went on to a triumphant end.

After the curtain had been rung down on the final tableau, she made a dash for the stairs to encounter Rowena ascending them. She had already donned her evening cape and scarf. At sight of Mignon she called out in the careless, good-humored fashion she could assume at will: "Hurry up. I'm going on out to the limousine. I need a breath of fresh air."

Partially convinced that Rowena had recovered from her fit of temper, Mignon gladly hastened to do her bidding. It was not until she began to look about for her high-laced boots that she changed her mind concerning her companion. They were nowhere to be seen. "Rowena has hidden them, just to be aggravating!" she exclaimed angrily. "That was her revenge. But I'll find them."

After a frantic ten-minutes' search she managed to locate them, tucked into either sleeve of the long fur coat she had worn. Thankful to find them, she laced them in a hurry and proceeded to dress with all speed. A repeated receding of footsteps and gay voices from the direction of the stairway warned her that the dressing rooms were being rapidly deserted. Those who had come to Riverview by railway had only a short time after the performance in which to catch the last train for the night.

Taking the stairs, two at a time, Mignon made a rush for the stage door and on out into the cold, starlit night. The first thing she noted was a large part of the cast hurriedly boarding a street car for the station. But where was the Farnham limousine and Rowena? Where was the little line of automobiles she had seen parked along the street when she entered the theatre? Only one now remained, almost a block farther up the street. Her heart beat thankfully as she observed it. It looked like the Farnham limousine. It was just like Rowena to thus draw away a little distance in order to scare her into thinking she had been left behind.

Racing toward it she saw that the chauffeur was engaged in examining one of its tires. She heard a cheery voice call out, "All right, Captain," and her knees grew weak. The voice did not sound like that of James, the Farnhams' chauffeur. Hoping against hope she came abreast of it. Then her elfin eyes grew wide with despair. It was not the Farnhams' car. It belonged to none other than the Deans.

Heartsick, she was about to turn away when a fresh young voice called out, "Mignon La Salle!" Forgetting everything except that she was in difficulties, she halted and managed to articulate, "Have you seen Miss Farnham's car?"

"Why, no," came the wondering reply. "Have you missed her?"

"I saw her go by in a limousine," stated Constance Stevens, from the tonneau of the Deans' car. "She was driving and the chauffeur was sitting beside her."

A belated light now dawned upon Mignon. She understood that this was the fruition of Rowena's threat. She had purposely run off and left her, knowing that she could not hope to catch the last train.

In the dark of the tonneau, Constance gave Marjorie's hand a quick pressure. Its instant return signified that her chum understood. Without hesitation she called to the tragic little figure on the sidewalk, "We'll take you home, Mignon. It's lucky that General stopped to examine that tire." Then to her father, "This is Mignon La Salle, Father. You know her, Mother."

"Yes." Mrs. Dean bowed in reserved fashion. "Get into the tonneau with the girls, Miss La Salle. We will see that you arrive safely at your own door."

The unexpected courtesy very nearly robbed the stranded girl of speech. Stammering her thanks, Mignon climbed ruefully into the tonneau and seated herself by Marjorie. As the car began a loud purr, preparatory to starting, her outraged feelings overcame her and she burst into tears. "It was hateful in her," she sobbed, "perfectly hateful."

"It was," agreed Marjorie positively. "But I wouldn't cry about it. You are all right now." Then with a view to cheering the weeper, she added: "You sang your part beautifully both nights, Mignon. That's something to be glad of. This little trouble doesn't really matter, since everything turned out well."

"It's nice in you to say it," quavered Mignon. "But, oh, how I despise that hateful, hateful girl. I'll never, never speak to her again as long as I live."

Marjorie might easily have assured her that this was a wise decision. Instead, she prudently refrained from committing herself. Mignon's mind continued to dwell on her wrongs. She cried and raged against her treacherous companion during most of the ride home. Constance and Marjorie were obliged to listen and administer judicious consolation. It did not appear to sink deep. Mignon was too self-centered to realize their generosity of spirit. When they left her at the La Salle's gate she tried to put graciousness into her thanks, but her thoughts were too firmly fixed upon faithless Rowena and herself to appreciate the kindness she had received.

"For once Mignon had to swallow a dose of her own medicine," commented Constance grimly, as the Deans' car sped away toward their home, where Connie was to spend the night with Marjorie.

"She found it pretty hard to take," mused Marjorie. "It's a good thing, though. This will end Mignon's friendship with Rowena, but it won't change her one little bit. I don't believe she'll ever change."

CHAPTER XXIII—A PECULIAR REQUEST

"Four letters for you, Lieutenant. Hunt them," decreed Mrs. Dean, as Marjorie burst into the living room, her cheeks rosy from the nipping kisses of the winter air.

"Oh, I know where they are." Jubilantly overturning the contents of her mother's sewing basket, she triumphantly drew them forth. Without bothering to remove her wraps she plumped down at her mother's feet to revel in her spoils.

"Here's one from Mary. I'll read that last. Here's one from Harriet." Opening it she read it through and passed it to her mother. "Harriet's almost well again. Isn't that good news? Why——" she had opened the next—"it's from Mignon; a little note of thanks. Oh, Captain!" she stared hard at the note. "I've discovered something. Mignon's not the horrid Observer. See. The writing and paper and all are quite different. I'm sure she isn't. She'd never ask anyone else to write such letters. It's not her way."

"Then that is good news, too," smiled Mrs. Dean. "I am also glad to know it. It is dreadful to misjudge anyone."

"I know that. I wish I knew who the Observer was, too." Marjorie sighed and took up the next letter. As she read it she laughed outright. "It's from General, the old dear. Just listen:

"Esteemed Lieutenant:

"Head up, forward march to the downtown barracks. Report for stern duty at : to-morrow (Thursday) P. M. Your most military presence is requested to assist in conferring with an official committee in a matter of great importance to the parties concerned. Failure to appear on time will be punished by court-martial. Be warned not to try to ambush your general in the living room to ascertain the facts beforehand. You will only be captured and sent to the guard house.

"Signed,

"General Dean."

"It's a surprise," nodded Marjorie. "I know it is. Very well, I'll show him that I'm not a bit curious. I'll tell him, though, that it's not fair to threaten a soldier. Do you know what it's about, Captain?"

"No; I am equally in the dark. I wouldn't tell you if I knew," Mrs. Dean answered teasingly.

"I wouldn't let you," retorted Marjorie. "I have to be loyal to my orders. Now I'll read Mary's letter and then go and answer it. If I don't answer it now I might put it off."

Laying the three notes aside, she busied herself with the long letter from Mary, reading it aloud with numerous exclamations and comments. True to her word, she made no mention to her father of his letter. Delighting to tease her, he hinted broadly concerning it, but failed to draw Marjorie into questioning him.

Nevertheless, it was a most curious young woman who entered his office the following afternoon at the exact moment of appointment. Her curiosity was lost in wide-eyed amazement as she saw that he was not alone. Seated in a chair beside his desk was a stout, dark man of middle age, whose restless, black eyes and small, dark mustache bespoke the foreigner. But this was not the cause of her astonishment. It lay in the fact that the man was Mignon La Salle's father. Both men rose as she entered, Mr. La Salle bowing to her in the graceful fashion of the Frenchman.

"Sit here, Lieutenant. Mr. La Salle wishes to talk with you. He is kind enough to allow me to be present at the conference."

"Miss Marjorie, I have not had the pleasure of meeting you before to-day. It is a very great pleasure. I have already thanked your father for his kindness to my daughter several evenings since. Now I must thank you, too. But I wish also to ask a far greater favor. My daughter, Mignon," he paused as though at a loss to proceed, "is a somewhat peculiar girl. For many years she has had no mother." He sighed, then continuing, "I wish her to be all that is good and fine. But I am a busy man. I cannot take time to be with her as I would desire. From my friend Harold Macy I have heard many pleasant things of you and your friends. So I have thought that it might be well to ask you if you——" Again he paused, his black eyes riveted on Marjorie, "if you will take an interest in my daughter, so that I may feel that her associates are of the best.

"I regret greatly her friendship with Miss Farnham. But that is past. She has told me all, and I have forbidden their further intimacy. Perhaps you are already the friend of my Mignon? If so, it is, indeed, well. If not, may I hope that you will soon become such, indeed?" There was a trace of pleading in his carefully enunciated speech with its slightly foreign accent.

A queer, choking sensation gripped Marjorie's throat. She was immeasurably touched. Happy in her General's love, she glimpsed something of the tender motive, which had actuated this stern man of business to plead for his daughter's welfare.

"I am willing to be Mignon's friend, if she is willing to be mine," she answered with grave sweetness. "I think I may speak for my friends, also."

"Thank you. She will respond, I am sure." A faint tightening of his thin lips gave hint that he would see to the exaction of that response. "It will be a pleasure to invite you to dine with us to-morrow evening," he added. La Salle Père evidently intended to allow no grass to grow under his feet.

"Thank you. May I go, General?" Marjorie's eyes sought her father's. Though she had maintained a gracious composure, he guessed that she was far from easy over this queer turn of affairs. There was a faintly martyred look in her brown eyes.

"Yes," he said in a steady, reassuring tone. "Your General approves." He flashed her a mischievous glance.

"Then you may expect me." Marjorie rose and offered her hand to the anxious father. "I must go now," she said. "I am very glad to have met you, Mr. La Salle."

Once outside the office she drew a long breath of dismay. "I'm quite sure of most of the girls," was her reflection, "but what, oh, what will Jerry say?"

CHAPTER XXIV—AN UNEXPECTED CALAMITY

Jerry had a great deal to say. She was so justly wrathful she very nearly cried. "It's the worst thing I ever heard of," she sputtered. "I wish we'd never revived that old operetta. Then Mignon wouldn't have sung in it and got left at the switch, and you wouldn't be asking us to make martyrs of ourselves. After all you've said about being through with Mignon, too! It's a shame!"

"But just suppose her father had come to you and asked you to help her, what would you have done?" pleaded Marjorie.

"Told him Mignon's history and advised him to lock her up," snapped Jerry. "I hope—— Oh, I don't know what I hope. I can't think of anything horrible enough to hope."

"Poor Jeremiah. It's too bad." Marjorie's little hand slipped itself into the plump girl's fingers. "You know you'd have done just as I did. I had quite a long talk with Mignon last night. After dinner her father left us to ourselves. It wasn't exactly pleasant. She would say mean things about Rowena. Still, she said she'd like to try again and wished that we would all help her. So I said for all of us that we would. You won't back out, will you, Jerry?"

"I don't know. Wait a week or two and see what she does, then I can tell better. You've got to show me. I mean, I must be convinced." Jerry wrinkled her nose at Marjorie and giggled. Her ruffled good humor was smoothing itself down.

"That means, you will help her," was Marjorie's fond translation. "Constance is willing, too. I am sure of Irma and Harriet, but Susan and Muriel are doubtful. Still, I think I can win them over if I tell them that you are with me in our plan."

"There's just this much about it, Marjorie." Jerry spoke with unusual seriousness. "Mignon will have to play fair or I'll drop her with a bang. Just like that. The first time I find her trying any of her deceitful tricks will be the last with me. Remember, I mean what I say. If anything like that happens, don't ask me to overlook it, for I won't. Not even to please you, and I'd rather please you than anybody else I know."

"I'll remember," laughed Marjorie. She was not greatly impressed by Jerry's declaration. The stout girl was apt to take a contrary stand, merely for the sake of variety. She had expected that Jerry would scold roundly, then give in with a final threatening grumble.

Susan and Muriel she found even harder to convince of Mignon's repentance than Jerry. Muriel was especially obstinate. "I'll speak to Mignon," she stipulated, "but I won't ask her to my house or go any place with her. Now that we've made over five hundred dollars out of the operetta for the library, you know we've been talking about getting up a club. Of course, she'll want to be in it. But she sha'n't."

"Then there's no use in trying to help her," said Marjorie calmly, "if we don't include her in our work and our good times."

"That's precisely what you said last year," retorted Muriel. "You invited her to your party and she nearly broke it up. After that I wonder that you can even dream of trusting her. I've known her longer than you, Marjorie. When we all went to grammar school together she was always the disturber. She used to fight with us and then come sliding around to make up. She'd promise to be good, but she never kept her word for long.

"Once she behaved pretty well for three months and we began to like her a little. Then one day some of us went to the woods on a picnic. We took our luncheon and spread a tablecloth on the grass. When we had all the eats spread out on the tablecloth and sat down around it, Mignon got mad because Susan said something to me that made me laugh. We happened to look at her, but we weren't talking about her. She thought so, though. She began sputtering at us like a firecracker. The more we all tried to calm her the madder she got. Before we could stop her she caught the tablecloth in both hands and gave it a hard jerk. You can imagine what happened! All our nice eats were jumbled together into the grass. The ants got into them and we had to throw nearly everything away. She didn't stop to help pick up things. She rushed off home and none of us spoke to her for the rest of the year. That's why I can't believe in her repentance. Sooner or later she's bound to upset things again, just as she did that time."

Marjorie could not resist laughing a little at Muriel's tragic tale of a woodland disaster. "I can't blame you for feeling as you do," she said, "but I must keep my word to her father. It means so much to him. Being in the operetta has given her a little start. Perhaps she's begun to see that it pays to do well. She knows now how it feels to be treated badly. It must remind her of some of the mean things she's done. If she's ever going to change, the time has come. But if no one believes in her, then she'll get discouraged and be worse than ever. Connie is willing to help. I'd be ashamed to refuse after that. Even Jerry says she'll consider it."

"Connie is a perfect angel, and Jerry is a goose," declared Muriel, flushing rather guiltily. It was difficult to continue to combat Marjorie's plan in the face of Constance's nobility of spirit. Constance had been the chief sufferer at Mignon's hands. Reminded of this, Muriel weakened. "I suppose I ought to get in line with Connie," she admitted. "I'd feel pretty small if I didn't. I can't afford to let Jerry beat me, either."

Muriel's objections thus overruled, Susan proved less hard to convince. Once more the reform party banded itself together to the performance of good works. Smarting from the effects of Rowena's cowardly spite, Mignon was quite willing to be taken up again by so important a set of girls as that to which Marjorie belonged. It pleased her not a little to know that she had gained a foothold that Rowena could never hope to win. Then, too, her father had taken a hand in her affairs. He had sternly informed her that she must about-face and do better. Relief at being plucked from a disagreeable situation, rather than gratitude toward her preservers, had predominated her feelings on the eventful night at Riverview. Fear of her father's threat to send her away to a convent school if she did not show rapid signs of improvement made her pause.

Returning from his business trip, Mr. La Salle had interviewed first William, the chauffeur, then Mignon. From an indulgent parent he became suddenly transformed into a stern inquisitor, before whose wrath Mignon broke down and haltingly confessed the truth. As a result he had forbidden her further acquaintance with Rowena. Reminded afresh of his parental duty, he had pondered long, then through the kindly offices of Mr. Dean, arranged the meeting with Marjorie. Thus Mignon's affairs had been readjusted and she had been forced to agree to follow the line of good conduct he had stretched for her.

It was a distinct relief, however, to Marjorie and her friends to find that Mignon was content to be merely on equitable terms. She did not try to force herself upon them, though she received whatever advances they made with an amiability quite unusual to her. They were immensely amused, however, at her frigid ignoring of Rowena Farnham. Her revenge consummated, Rowena decided to re-assume her sway over her unwilling follower. Mignon fiercely declined to be reinstated and the two held a battle royal in which words became sharpest arrows. Later, Rowena was plunged into fresh rage by the news that Mignon had been taken up by the very girls she had over and over again disparaged.

Determined not to be beaten, she continued to waylay Mignon as she went to and from school. Changing her bullying tactics, she next tried coaxing. But Mignon maintained her air of virtuous frigidity and took an especial delight in snubbing the girl she had once feared. It also gave her infinite pleasure to paint Rowena in exceedingly dark colors to whomever would listen to her grievances. Much of this came in round-about fashion to the reformers. They disapproved of it intensely, but held their peace rather than undo the little good they hoped they had already accomplished.

Among her schoolmates the account of Mignon's near misfortune was received with varying degrees of interest. A few were sympathetically disposed; others merely laughed. Rowena, however, lost caste. Neither her costly clothes, her caustic wit nor her impudently fascinating personality could cover the fact that she had done a treacherous and contemptible deed. The fact that she had left a young girl stranded at midnight in a strange town did not add to her doubtful popularity. Quick to discover this state of affairs, she realized that she had gone a step too far. There was only one way in which she might redeem herself and that lay in the direction of basket ball.

February was speedily living out his short, changeable life. The third of the four games between the sophomore-junior teams was to be played on the last Saturday afternoon of the month, which fell on the twenty-seventh. Thus far each side had won a game. Rowena decreed that the two games yet to be played should go to the sophomores. She would play as she had never played before. Nothing should stand in her way. She would lead the sophomores on to glory and the acclamation of her class would cleanse her blurred escutcheon. Once she had re-established her power she would make Mignon sorry.

Fortunately for her plans, the members of her team had showed no great amount of prejudice against her since the affair of the operetta. They treated her cordially enough during practice and applauded her clever playing. Shrewd to a degree, she divined instantly that they cherished no special regard for her. They were simply using her as a means to the end. Knowing her value as a player, they were egging her on to do well because of their hope of victory in the next two games. She did not doubt that when the season was over there would be a general falling-off in their cordiality unless she so greatly distinguished herself as to win their ungrudging admiration.

Alas for her dream of power, when the third game came off between the two teams, it was the juniors who carried off the palm with a score of - in their favor. What galled her most was the remarkably brilliant playing of Marjorie Dean. If there lingered a doubt in the mind of Miss Davis regarding Marjorie's ability to play basket ball, her work on the floor that Saturday afternoon must have completely discounted that doubt. What Miss Davis thought when, from the gallery, she watched the clever playing of the girl she had endeavored to dismiss from the team, was something which was recorded only on her own brain. It was noted by several pairs of watchful eyes that she did not applaud the victors. She had not forgiven them for the difficulties into which they had plunged her on that fateful afternoon.

Losing the game to the enemy made matters distinctly mortifying for Rowena. Among themselves, her teammates gloomily conceded that they had over-rated her as a player. Though they made some effort to conceal their resentment, their cordiality became less apparent. This second defeat precluded all hope of doing more than tying the score in the one game still to be played. They needed Rowena's help to bring about that result. Therefore, they dared not express themselves openly. It may be recorded here that the ideals of the four sophomore players were no higher than those of Rowena. Their attitude toward her was glaringly selfish and they were possessed of little loyalty.

The final game was set for the thirteenth of March. Doggedly bent on escaping a whitewashing, the sophomores devoted themselves to zealous practice. So insistently frequent were their demands for the use of the gymnasium that the junior team were obliged to make equally insistent protest against their encroachment.

"I am really glad that this next game is to be the last," remarked Marjorie to her teammates one afternoon as they were preparing to leave the dressing room after practice. "Basket ball hasn't seemed the same old game this year. Perhaps I'm outgrowing my liking for it, but really we've had so much trouble about it that I long for victory and peace."

"It's not the game," contested Muriel. "It's those sophs with Rowena Farnham leading them on. Why, even when Mignon was continually fussing with us we never had any trouble about getting the gym for practice. Oh, well, one week from to-morrow will tell the story. If we win it will be a three to one victory. We can't lose now. All the sophs can do is to tie the score."

"Where were our subs to-day?" demanded Daisy Griggs. "I didn't see either of them."

"Harriet couldn't stay for practice. She was going to a tea with her mother," informed Susan. "I don't know where Lucy Warner was. I didn't see her in school, either."

"She must be sick. She hasn't been in school for almost a week," commented Muriel. "She is the queerest-acting girl. You'd think to look at her that she hated herself and everybody. She makes me think of a picture of an anarchist I once saw in a newspaper. When she does come to practice she just sits with her chin in her hands and glowers. I can't understand how she ever happened to come out of her grouch long enough to make the team."

"She's awfully distant," agreed Marjorie dispiritedly. "I have tried to be nice to her, but it's no use. My, how the wind howls! Listen." Going to the window of the dressing room, she peered out. "It's a dreadful day. The walks are solid sheets of ice. The wind blew so hard I could scarcely keep on my feet this noon."

"I fell down twice," giggled Susan Atwell. "It didn't hurt me much. I scraped one hand on a piece of sharp ice, but I'm still alive."

"Be careful going down the steps," warned Daisy Griggs, ever a youthful calamity howler.

"Don't croak, Daisy. If you keep on someone will take a tumble just because you mentioned it," laughed Muriel. "We can't afford that with the game so near."

Dressed at last, their paraphernalia carefully stowed away, the team trooped from the gymnasium and on to their locker room. "I wish I had worn my fur coat," lamented Muriel. "I'll surely freeze in my tracks. Are you ready, girls? Do hurry. I am anxious to face the wind and get it over with. I think I'll take the car home."

"Ugh!" shuddered Susan. Issuing from the high school building a blast of piercing air struck her full in the face. "We'll be blown away before we get down the steps."

"Oh, come along, Susie," urged Muriel laughingly. "Don't mind a little thing like that. Look at me. Here goes." Muriel valiantly essayed the first icy step. A fresh gust of wind assailing her, the hand holding her muff sought her face to protect it.

How it happened no one quite knew. A concerted scream went up from four throats as Muriel suddenly left her feet to go bumping and sliding down the long flight of ice-bound steps. She struck the walk in a heap and lay still.

"Muriel!" Forgetting the peril of the steps, Marjorie took them heedlessly, but safely. A faint moan issued from Muriel's lips as she knelt beside her. Muriel moaned again, but tried to raise herself to a sitting posture. She fell back with a fresh groan.

"Where are you hurt?" Marjorie slipped a supporting arm under her. By this time the others had safely made the descent and were gathered about the two.

"It's my right shoulder and arm. I'm afraid my arm is broken," gasped Muriel, her face white with pain.

"Let me see." Marjorie tenderly felt of the injured member. "Do I hurt you much?" she quavered solicitously.

"Not—much. I guess it's—not—broken. It's my shoulder that hurts most."

Several persons had now gathered to the scene. A man driving past in an automobile halted his car. Leaping from the machine he ran to the scene. "Someone hurt?" was his crisp question. "Can I be of service?"

"Oh, if you would." Marjorie's face brightened. "Miss Harding fell down those steps. She's badly hurt."

"Where does she live? I'll take her home," offered the kindly motorist. Lifting Muriel in his arms he carried her to the car and gently deposited her in its tonneau. "Perhaps you'd better come with her," he suggested.

"Thank you, I will. Good-bye, girls. Go on over to my house and wait for me. I'll be there in a little while." Lifting her hand to the three frightened girls, who had advanced upon the machine with sundry other curious pedestrians, Marjorie gave Muriel's rescuer the Hardings' address, climbed into the car and slammed the door shut.

"Poor Muriel," wailed Daisy Griggs, as the car rolled away. "I told her to be careful. I hope she isn't hurt much. And the game next week!"

Three pairs of startled eyes met and conveyed the same dismaying thought. What would the team do without Captain Muriel?

CHAPTER XXV—A STRENUOUS HIKE TO A TRYING ENGAGEMENT

Everybody knows the trite saying: "It never rains but that it pours." The disasters of the following week seemed quite in accord with it. Muriel's spectacular slide down the ice steps brought her a broken collarbone. The three anxious girls had awaited news of Muriel at Marjorie's home had hardly taken their leave when the ring of the postman brought her fresh misery. Little knowing what he did, that patient individual handed Marjorie a letter which filled her with angry consternation. Why in the world had the hated Observer come to life again at such a time?

Without waiting to read the unwelcome epistle in her Captain's presence, Marjorie ripped open the envelope with a savage hand. This time the unknown was detestably brief, writing merely:

"Miss Dean:

"I hope you lose the game next Saturday. You are more of a snob than ever. Defeat will do you good. Prepare to meet it.

"The Observer."

"Oh!" Marjorie dashed the offending letter to the floor. Muriel's accident was bad enough. It had not needed this to complete her dejection. Recapturing the spiteful message she was about to tear it into bits. On second reflection she decided to keep it and add it to her obnoxious collection. Something whispered to her that the identity of the tormenting Observer would yet be revealed to her.

Facing the lamentable knowledge that Muriel must be counted out of the coming contest, Harriet replaced her. This in itself provided a grain of comfort. Harriet was a skilful player and would work for the success of the team with all her energy. The other four players congratulated themselves on thus having such able support. Due to Muriel's absence, Marjorie had been asked to assume temporary captainship. Her mind now at ease by reason of Harriet's good work, she gave her most conscientious attention to practice.

Matters skimmed along with commendable smoothness until the Wednesday before the game. Then she encountered a fresh set-back. Word came to her that Susan Atwell had succumbed to the dreaded tonsilitis that all through the winter had been going its deadly round in Sanford. On receipt of the news she recalled that for the past two days Susan had complained of sore throat. She had given it no serious thought, however. Her own throat had also troubled her a trifle since that stormy day when Muriel had come to grief. There was but one thing to do. Put Lucy Warner in Susan's position. Her heart almost skipped a beat as she faced the fact that Lucy, too, had been absent from school for over a week. Someone had said that Lucy was also ill. Marjorie reproached herself for not having inquired more closely about the peculiar green-eyed junior. "I ought to have gone to see her," she reflected. "I'll go to-night. Perhaps she is almost well by this time, and can come back to school in time for the game. If she can't, then I'd better ask Mignon to play in Susan's place."

School over for the day she accosted Jerry and Irma with, "I can only walk as far as the corner with you to-night. I'm going to see Lucy Warner. She's been sick for over a week. Did you ever hear of such bad luck as the team has been having lately? I feel so discouraged and tired out. I don't believe I'll try for the team next year." Marjorie's usually sprightliness was entirely missing. Her voice had taken on a weary tone and her brown eyes had lost their pretty sparkle.

"You'd better go straight home and take care of yourself," gruffly advised Jerry, "or you won't be fit to play on the team Saturday."

"Oh, I'm all right." Marjorie made an attempt to look cheerful. "I'm not feeling ill. My throat is a little bit sore. I caught cold that day Muriel fell down the steps. But it's nothing serious. I shall go to bed at eight o'clock to-night and have a long sleep. I'm just tired; not sick. I must leave you here. Good-bye. See you to-morrow." Nodding brightly she left the two and turned down a side street.

"See us to-morrow," sniffed Jerry. "Humph! I doubt it, unless we go to her house. She's about half sick now. It's the first time I ever saw her look that way. She's so brave, though. She'd fight to keep up if she were dying."

Meanwhile, as she plodded down the snowy street on her errand of mercy, Marjorie was, indeed, fighting to make herself believe that she was merely a little tired. Despite her languor, generosity prompted her to stop in passing a fruit store and purchase an attractive basket filled with various fruits likely to tempt the appetite of a sick person. She wondered if Lucy would resent the offering. She was such a queer, self-contained little creature.

"What a dingy house!" was her thought, as she floundered her way through a stretch of deep snow to Lucy's unpretentious home. Detached from its neighbors, it stood unfenced, facing a bit of field, which the small boys of Sanford used in summer as a ball ground. It was across this field that Marjorie was obliged to wend a course made difficult by a week's fall of snow that blanketed it. An irregular path made by the passing and repassing of someone's feet led up to the door. It appeared that the Warners were either too busy or else unable to clear their walk.

Finding no bell, Marjorie removed her glove and knocked on the weather-stained front door. It was opened by a frail little woman with a white, tired face and faded blue eyes. She stared in amazement at the trim, fur-coated girl before her, whose attractive appearance betokened affluence. "How do you do?" she greeted in evident embarrassment.

"Good afternoon. Are you Mrs. Warner?" Marjorie asked brightly. "I have come to see Lucy. How is she to-day? I am Marjorie Dean."

"Oh, are you Miss Dean? I mailed a letter she wrote you several days ago. Come in, please," invited the woman cordially. "I am very glad to see you. I am sure Lucy will be. She is better but still in bed. Will you take off your wraps?"

"No, thank you. I can't stay very long. I feel guilty at not coming to see her sooner. What is the trouble with her—tonsilitis? So many people in Sanford are having it." Marjorie looked slightly mystified over Mrs. Warner's reference to the letter. She had received no letter from Lucy. She decided, however, that she would ask Lucy.

"No; she was threatened with pneumonia, but managed to escape with a severe cold. I will take you to her. She is upstairs."

Following Mrs. Warner up a narrow stairway that led up from a bare, cheerless sitting room, Marjorie was forced to contrast the dismal place with the Deans' luxurious living room. Why was it, she sadly pondered, that she had been given so much and Lucy so little? The Warners' home was even more poverty-stricken than the little gray house in which Constance Stevens had once lived. Then she had deplored that same contrast between herself and Constance.

"Miss Dean has come to see you, Lucy," said Mrs. Warner. Marjorie had followed the woman into a plain little bedroom, equally bare and desolate.

"You!" Glimpsing Marjorie behind her mother, Lucy sat up in bed, her green eyes growing greener with horrified disapproval.

"Yes, I." Marjorie flushed as she strove to answer playfully. That single unfriendly word of greeting had wounded her deeply. The very fact that, half sick herself, she had waded through the snow to call on Lucy gave her a fleeting sense of injury. She tried to hide it by quickly saying: "I must apologize for not visiting you sooner. Our team has had so many mishaps, I have been busy trying to keep things going. I brought you some fruit to cheer you up."

"I will leave you girls to yourselves," broke in Mrs. Warner. As she went downstairs she wondered at her daughter's ungracious behavior to this lovely young friend. Lucy was such a strange child. Even she could not always fathom her odd ways.

"Why have you come to see me?" demanded Lucy, hostile and inhospitable. All the time her lambent green eyes remained fixed upon Marjorie.

"Why shouldn't I come to see you?" Marjorie gave a nervous little laugh. Privately she wished she had not come. Embarrassment at the unfriendly reception drove the question of the letter from her mind.

"You never noticed me in school," pursued Lucy relentlessly. "Why should you now?"

"You would never let me be friends with you," was Marjorie's honest retort. "I've tried ever so many times. I have always admired you. You are so bright and make such brilliant recitations."

"What does that matter when one is poor and always out of things?" came the bitter question.

"Oh, being poor doesn't count. It's the real you that makes the difference. When I was a little girl we were quite poor. We aren't rich now; just in comfortable circumstances. If I chose my friends for their money I'd be a very contemptible person. You mustn't look at matters in that light. It's wrong. It shuts you away from all the best things in life; like love and friendship and contentment. I wish you had said this to me long ago. Then we would have understood each other and been friends."

"I can never be your friend," stated the girl solemnly.

"Why not?" Marjorie's eyes widened. "Perhaps I ought not to ask you that. It sounded conceited. I can't blame you if you don't like me. There are many persons I can't like, either. Sometimes I try to like them, but I seldom succeed," she made frank admission.

"You are a puzzling girl," asserted Lucy, her green eyes wavering under Marjorie's sweetly naïve confession. "Either you are very deceitful, or else I have made a terrible mistake." She suddenly lay back in bed, half hiding her brown head in the pillow.

"I would rather think that you had made a mistake." The rose in Marjorie's cheeks deepened. "I try never to be deceitful."

Lucy did not reply, but buried her face deeper in the pillow. An oppressive silence ensued, during which Marjorie racked her brain as to what she had best say next. What ailed Lucy? She was even queerer than Marjorie had supposed.

With a convulsive jerk Lucy suddenly sat upright. Marjorie was relieved to observe no indication of tears in the probing green eyes. She had feared Lucy might be crying. Why she should cry was a mystery, however.

"If you had made a mistake about someone and then done a perfectly dreadful thing and afterward found out that it was all a mistake, what would you do?" Lucy queried with nervous intensity.

"I—that's a hard question to answer. It would depend a good deal on what I had done and who the person was."

"But if the person didn't know that it was you who did it, would you tell them?" continued Lucy.

"If I had hurt them very much, I think my conscience would torment me until I did," Marjorie said slowly. "It would be hard, of course, but it would be exactly what I deserved. But why do you ask me such strange things?"

"Because I must know. I've done something wrong and I've got to face it. I've just found out that I have a very lively conscience. What you said is true. I deserve to suffer. I am the Observer." Lucy dropped back on her pillow, her long, black lashes veiling her peculiarly colored eyes.

Undiluted amazement tied Marjorie's tongue. Staring at the pitifully white, small face against the pillow, she came into a flashing, emotional knowledge of the embittered spirit that had prompted the writing of those vexatious letters. "You poor little thing!" she cried out compassionately. The next instant her soft hands held one of Lucy's in a caressing clasp.

Lucy's heavy lids lifted. "I don't wonder your friends love you," she said somberly. Her free hand came to rest lightly on Marjorie's arm. "I know now that I could have been your friend, too."

"But you shall be from this minute on," Marjorie replied, her pretty face divinely tender. "You've proved your right to be. It was brave in you to tell me. If you hadn't been the right sort of girl you might have decided to like me and kept what you told me to yourself. I would never have known the difference. I am glad that I do know. It takes away the shadow. I understand that you must have suffered a great deal. I blame myself, too. I'm afraid I've thought too much about my own pleasure and seemed snobbish."

"I wouldn't have done it, only one Sunday when you were walking along with that Miss Macy and that girl who used to live at your house, I met you and you didn't speak to me. All three of you were dressed beautifully. It made me feel so bad. I was wearing an old gray suit, and I thought you cut me on account of my clothes. I know now that I was wrong. That was the beginning of the mistake. Then when you girls had those expensive basket ball suits made, I thought you chose them just to be mean to me. Of course, I didn't expect to be invited to your parties, but it hurt me to be passed by all the time in school."

"I never saw you that day, and I'm sure we never thought about how it might look to others when we ordered our suits. You've taught me a lesson, Lucy. One ought to be made careful about such things in a large school. Someone is sure to be made unhappy. Now we must put all the bad things away for good and think only of the nice ones. When you get well you are going to have some good times with me. My friends will like you, too. No one must ever know about—well, about the mistake."

But Lucy could not thus easily take things for granted. Remorse had set in and she felt that she ought to be punished for her fault. After considerable cheerful persuasion, Marjorie brought her into an easier frame of mind. When finally she said good-bye she left behind her a most humble Observer who had given her word thereafter to observe life from a happier angle.

Once away from the house a feeling of heavy lassitude overwhelmed the patient Lieutenant. It had been a strenuous hike to a trying engagement. Her head swam dizzily as she stumbled through the drifted field to better walking. Her wet shoes and stockings added to her misery. How her cheeks burned and how dreadfully her throat ached! Was Jerry's prediction about to be fulfilled? Was she only tired out, or had actual sickness descended upon her just when she needed most to be well?

CHAPTER XXVI—"TURN ABOUT IS FAIR PLAY"

"What did I tell you yesterday?" saluted Jerry Macy, the instant she found opportunity to address Irma Linton the next morning. "Marjorie's sick. Her mother telephoned me before I started for school. She came from Lucy Warner's yesterday so sick she couldn't see straight. Her mother put her to bed and sent for the doctor. She has tonsilitis. Isn't that hard luck?"

"I should say so. Poor Marjorie. I was afraid of that yesterday. You know she said her throat was sore." Irma looked unutterably sympathetic. "And the game on Saturday, too. But it can't be played with Marjorie, Muriel and Susan all laid up. That leaves only Rita, Daisy and Harriet on the team."

"The sophomores will have to call it off," decreed Jerry. "It's only fair. The juniors did that very thing when two of the sophs were sick."

"You'd better see Ellen this noon or before, if you can, and tell her," Irma advised. "Then she can break it to the sophs to-day."

"I'm going to wait for her in the senior locker room this noon," nodded Jerry. "Then she can post a notice at once. Now I must beat it for Cæsar recitation. I wished he'd been killed in his first battle. It would have saved me a good deal of bother." Jerry's jolly chuckle belied her vengeful comment on the valorous general.

"You don't say so!" exclaimed Ellen when Jerry broke the news to her. "That is too bad. Certainly the game will have to be postponed. I'll write a notice instantly asking the sophs to meet me in the gym at four this afternoon. I must call up on the 'phone and inquire for Marjorie. Dear little girl, I wish I could do a great deal more for her. Thank you for telling me, Jerry." Ellen hurried off to write and then post the notice before going home to luncheon. Her lips wore a quizzical smile. She wondered what the sophomore team would say when she told them.

She had just finished tucking it into the bulletin board when Nellie Simmons, a member of the sophomore team, paused curiously to read it. The very fact that it came from Ellen's hands indicated basket ball news. "Hmm!" she ejaculated as she took in its contents. "What's the matter now?"

"I'll tell you at four o'clock," Ellen flashed back. With a slight lift of her shoulders, she walked away. Nellie's tone had verged on the insolent. She had hardly disappeared when Nellie faced about and hurried toward the sophomore locker room, bumping smartly against Rowena Farnham, who was in the act of leaving it.

"Look out!" cried Rowena. "What are you trying to do? I'm not made of iron."

"Oh, Rowena, I was hurrying to find you!" exclaimed Nellie. "Ellen Seymour just posted a notice on the bulletin board for the team to meet her in the gym at four o'clock. I think I know what it's about. Marjorie Dean is sick. I heard Jerry Macy tell Esther Lind. You know what that means to the junior team, with two others away from it. I'm sure Ellen's going to ask us to postpone the game."

"I'll forgive you for almost knocking me down," laughed Rowena, her black eyes glowing. "So Miss Seymour thinks we will postpone the game to please her and that goody-goody Dean girl. I'll see that she gets a surprise. Lucky you came to me. I can fix things before I go home to luncheon. I'm going to have a talk with Miss Davis."

Leaving Nellie plunged in admiration at her daring tactics, Rowena sped up the basement stairs and down the corridor toward Miss Davis's tiny office. "How are you, Miss Davis?" was her offhand greeting. "I've come to you for help."

Miss Davis viewed her visitor with mild disapproval. "I don't care to implicate myself in any more of your tangles, Rowena," she declared firmly.

"Oh, this isn't entirely my affair. It's about basket ball, though. That Dean girl is sick and Miss Seymour is going to ask us to postpone the game just on her account. Of course, we'll say 'no,' but Miss Seymour won't mind that unless you stand by us. It's pure favoritism. Miss Harding and Miss Atwell are sick, too. Even so, there are three of the team left. If you say the game must go on, it will give poor Mignon a chance to sub in the Dean girl's place. That Esther Lind played on the sophomore team last year. She could fill the other position and we could have the game. Miss Seymour knows that, but she won't pay any attention to it. Mignon ought to have been chosen in the first place. You owe it to her to do this for her. Besides, it will give you a good chance to even things with the Seymour-Dean combination."

"I don't like your tone, Rowena. It's hardly respectful. As a teacher I have no desire to 'even things,' as you express it." Miss Davis's censure did not ring true. She knew that this domineering girl had no illusions concerning her dignity of position.

Rowena merely smiled in the bold, cheerful fashion that she always adopted and which passed for real good humor. She did not take Miss Davis at her word. "Think it over," she advised. "You know you detest favoritism." She was well aware that Miss Davis deplored it, only to practise it as regarded herself and Mignon. Mignon in particular had always ranked high in her favor.

To have heard Rowena thus pleading her cause would have astonished Mignon not a little. It was by this very means that Rowena proposed to seek her and win back the French girl's allegiance. Without her companionship, school had become very tame for lawless Rowena.

"When is this meeting to take place?" asked Miss Davis with well-simulated indifference.

"At four o'clock." Rowena thrilled with triumph. She knew she had gained her point.

"I may attend it," was the teacher's vague promise.

"Thank you. I hope for Mignon's sake you'll be there." With this sly reminder Rowena set off, determining to waylay Mignon on her walk back from luncheon. Not troubling to go home that noon, Rowena swallowed a hasty luncheon at a nearby delicatessen shop and posted herself at a corner, which Mignon was due to pass.

"Wait a minute, Mignon," she hailed, as the latter was about to pass her by with a haughty toss of her head. "You must listen to me. I've just fixed it for you to play on the junior team Saturday."

Astounded by this remarkable statement, Mignon halted. Rowena had guessed that she would. "I don't understand you," she said haughtily.

"Yes, you do," assured Rowena blithely. "Three of the juniors are sick. I just asked Miss Davis to let you help out. She is going to see Miss Seymour about it this afternoon. All you have to do is to keep still until you're asked to play, then say 'yes.' Now do you believe I'm your friend?" she concluded in triumph.

Mignon's inimitable shrug went into play. "You are very kind," she returned with a trace of sarcasm. "It's about time you did something to make up for all the trouble you caused me."

"That's just it." Rowena clutched at this providential straw, which Mignon had unwittingly cast to her. "I am trying to make it up to you. I won't bother you any more now. But I hope——" she paused significantly.

"You may walk to school with me," graciously permitted Mignon. The old fascination of Rowena's lawlessness was beginning to steal over her.

"Thank you." Rowena spoke humbly. Inwardly she was jubilant. She was obliged to endure these stupid persons, but they were all her pawns, willed to move about at her dictation.

After she had left Rowena in the corridor, Mignon indulged in sober speculation. There was more to the affair than appeared on the surface. Formerly she would have entered into it with avidity. Now she was bound to respect her father's mandate or be packed off to a convent school. She alone knew positively that recent association with Marjorie and her chums had not changed her. But she must make a pretense at keeping up an appearance of amiable docility. Rowena's words still sounded in her ears like a clarion call to battle. But she was resolved to do nothing rash. She would wait and see before accepting the chance to play on the junior team. It was lucky that she need not lend her presence to the meeting that afternoon.

When at four o'clock Ellen Seymour put the matter of postponement to five impassive-faced girls, she was not greatly surprised to listen to their unanimous refusal to consider the proposal. One and all they stolidly set themselves against it.

"You forget that the juniors treated you very nicely when your team met with misfortune," reminded Ellen gravely. She had vowed within herself that she would not lose her temper.

This reminder brought stubborn replies of, "That was different," and "They have plenty of equally good players to draw from."

In the midst of the discussion, Miss Davis appeared on the scene. Ellen understood only too well what that meant. "What seems to be the matter here?" she asked. "Are you discussing the question of postponing the game?"

Rowena cast a sidelong glance of triumph toward Nellie Simmons, which said: "What did I tell you?"

"We are," was Ellen's crisp return. "The game must be postponed."

It was an unlucky speech on Ellen's part. Miss Davis had entered the gymnasium only half decided upon championing Rowena's cause. The cool decision in the senior's tones angered her. "I hardly think that will be necessary," she retorted. "Three of the juniors are ready to play. Miss La Salle and Miss Lind can substitute for the others. The game will go forward on Saturday."

"That is absolutely unfair," cried Ellen. "The juniors were extremely lenient with——"

"That will do." Miss Davis held up an authoritative hand. "Another word and I will report you to Miss Archer. Then there will be no game on Saturday."

Ellen did not answer this threat. Her head erect, color high, she walked from the gymnasium and straight to Miss Archer's office. She had not threatened. She intended to act and act quickly.

"Miss Archer, I have something important to say to you," she burst forth on entering the principal's office.

"Sit down, Ellen. I am sure it must be. Don't tell me it is basket ball!" Miss Archer's lips tightened.

"But it is." Impetuously, Ellen poured forth her story. When she had finished, Miss Archer's face was not good to see.

"I'll attend to this, Ellen. You did right to come to me. There will be no game on Saturday."

The following morning five girls received a summons to the principal's office that put fear into their hearts. When, one by one, they appeared, she motioned them to be seated until the last one had completed the line on the oak bench. Swinging in her chair, she faced them with: "There is an old saying, girls, 'Turn about is fair play.' Since you seem to have forgotten it, I am forced to remind you. I understand that you asked the juniors to postpone the first basket ball game of the season, due to the fact that your team was temporarily incapacitated. They did so. That in itself points to an adherence to fair play. Very well. Now there comes a time when the situation reverses itself. Having proved themselves honorable, the juniors have called for a like demonstration of honor on the part of the sophomores. You know best what has happened. You have shown yourselves not only grossly ungrateful, but unfit to be trusted. No one enjoys dealing with ingrates. One understands precisely what one may expect from such persons.

"During the year I have not been pleased with the various reports which have been brought to me concerning sophomore and junior basket ball; particularly sophomore basket ball. It is not long since I was obliged to interfere with sophomore methods. At that time I stated that a repetition of such unfair tactics would result in the stoppage of the game for the rest of the year. I now declare the sophomore and junior teams disbanded. There will be no more games between them this year. I have just one thing further to say. It is unfortunate that the innocent should be obliged to suffer with the guilty. You are dismissed."

A wavering breath of dismay passed along the row of girls as Miss Archer pronounced sentence upon them. Their own treachery had proved a boomerang. Dejection laid heavy hand upon four of them, as with downcast eyes they rose and quitted the place of judgment. But the fifth member of the disbanded team was not thus so easily dismissed. Far from disheartened, Rowena Farnham sprang forward, hands clenched at her sides, her face an angry flame.

"Who are you that you dare talk of unfairness?" In her devouring rage she fairly screamed the question. "You have disbanded the team just to please that smug-faced, priggish Marjorie Dean. You are not fit to have charge over a school of girls. I am ashamed to be under the same roof with you. I shall ask my father——"

"It strikes me that it is I who should inform your father of your outrageous behavior to me," interrupted Miss Archer in a stern voice. "I hardly believe that he would countenance such impudence on your part to one in authority over you. You may go home and remain away from school until I send for you. I shall insist on an interview with your father at the earliest possible moment in order to decide what is to be done with you."

"You won't have to insist on seeing him," sneered Rowena. "He will call on you this afternoon. My father won't see me abused by you. He will use his influence with the Board of Education. Then you won't be principal of Sanford High School." With this furious prediction of downfall Rowena flung herself out of the office, confident that she had delivered a telling thrust. Not daring to return to the study hall she sped to the locker room, hastily seized her wraps and departed for her father's office in high dudgeon.

The brilliantly-colored account of Miss Archer's misdeeds which she poured into the ears of her too-credulous father sent him on the trail of the offending principal with fury in his eye. Less than an hour after Rowena had made her sensational exit, a very tall, red-haired, red-faced man stalked into Miss Archer's office with the air of a blood-thirsty warrior.

"Madam," he thundered, omitting polite preliminaries, "I am Mr. Farnham and I wish you to understand most emphatically that you cannot criticize my methods of bringing up my daughter. Though she may need occasional mild discipline it is extreme bad taste in you to cast unjust reflections upon her parents."

"I was not aware that I had done so." Miss Archer had risen to confront the slandered (?) parent. She met his angry gaze unflinchingly. "I had intended to send for you, however. Now that you are here we may as well settle matters at once. Your daughter——"

"My daughter has been shamefully abused," cut in Mr. Farnham majestically. "I regret that I ever allowed her to enter a public school. I shall remove her at once from it. The contaminating influence——"

It was Miss Archer's turn to interrupt in clear, cutting speech. "Allow me to amend your last statement to her contaminating influence. Your daughter is a trouble-maker. I have borne very patiently with her. I cannot regret your decision to remove her from Sanford High School. It simplifies matters immeasurably."

Miss Archer's quiet, but intense utterance sent an unbidden thrill of consternation over the irate man. His blustering manner had not intimidated this regal, calm-featured woman. He experienced a sudden sense of defeat. Fearful lest he might reveal it, he cut his call short with, "My daughter will not return to school. Good morning."

Miss Archer bowed him out, feeling sorry rather than displeased with the big, blustering man whom fatherly love had blinded to his daughter's faults. She wondered when, if ever, his eyes would be opened. Under what circumstances would he awaken to full knowledge of the real Rowena?

CHAPTER XXVII—THE FIRST DUTY OF A SOLDIER

"And we can have the party in her room? Oh, fine! You're awfully dear, Mrs. Dean. We'll be there at two this afternoon. Good-bye." Jerry Macy hung up the telephone receiver and did an energetic dance about the hall.

"Training for the Russian Ballet?" asked Hal, as, emerging from the breakfast room, he beheld Jerry in the midst of her weird dance.

"No, you goose. I'm doing a dance of rejoicing. Marjorie's well enough to see us. We are going to have a party for her this afternoon."

"You are a lovely girl, Jerry, and you dance beautifully." Hal became suddenly ingratiating. "Am I invited to the party?"

"Certainly not. It's an exclusive affair; no boys allowed. You may send Marjorie some flowers, though. You've only sent them twice this week."

"I'll do it. What time is the party?"

"Two o'clock. Get them at Braley's. That's the nicest place." Jerry was obliged to shout this last after Hal, as, seizing his cap and coat, he raced out the front door.

Over two weeks had elapsed since the Thursday morning which had marked the downfall of basket ball. During that time, Marjorie had lain in her dainty pink-and-white bed, impatiently wondering if she were ever going to get well. But one thing had helped to make her trying illness endurable. Never before had she realized that she had so many friends. Her pretty "house" looked like a florist's shop and her willow table was piled with offerings of fruit and confectionery sent her by her devoted followers. Every day the mail brought her relays of cheery letters, the burden of which was invariably, "You must hurry and get well."

And now the day of convalescence had dawned. She was able not only to sit up, but to take brief strolls about her room. Her faithful Captain had just brought her word that Jerry and the girls would be with her that afternoon. What a lot they would have to talk about! Marjorie lay luxuriously back among her pillows and smilingly patted a fat letter from Mary Raymond. "How I wish you could be here, too, Lieutenant," she murmured. "We need you to help us with our good time. Connie's coming over early to help Captain dress me in my wonderful new pink negligee. It has ruffles and ruffles. I wish you could see it, Mary."

"You are only playing invalid," laughingly accused Constance Stevens. It was a little after one o'clock. She and Mrs. Dean had just finished arraying Marjorie in the half-fitted pink silk negligee that had been one of Captain's cheer-up gifts to her. "I never before saw you look so pretty, Marjorie," she declared, as she stepped back to view the effect. "You ought always to wear your hair down your back in long curls."

"Just imagine how I'd look. And I so nearly a senior, too. Connie, do you suppose Mignon will come to my party?" Marjorie asked with sudden irrelevance.

"When I invited her to it she said she'd come," returned Constance. "You can't tell much about her, though. The day before Miss Archer forbade basket ball I saw Rowena stop her and walk into school with her. I thought it rather queer. She had said so much against Rowena after that night at Riverview."

"She is a strange girl," mused Marjorie. "I am not very sorry that Rowena Farnham has left high school. Judging from what you just said, it wouldn't have been long until they grew chummy again. Rowena would have found a way to win Mignon over to her."

In making this prediction Marjorie had spoken more accurately than she knew. Emboldened by her success in once more attracting Mignon's attention to herself, Rowena had planned to follow that move with others equally strategic. But before she had found opportunity for a second interview, basket ball had been doomed and she had ceased to be a pupil of Sanford High.

Being among the first to get wind of Miss Archer's decree and Rowena's exodus from school, Mignon secretly rejoiced in the thought that she had not been implicated in the affair. She had fully made up her mind to accept the invitation to play on the junior team, were it extended to her. When she discovered the true state of matters, she made haste to declare openly that had she been asked, nothing would have induced her to accept the offer. As for Rowena, she should have known better. After the shabby treatment she had received from Rowena, it was ridiculous in her to dream that she, Mignon, would lend herself to anything so contemptible. A few such guileful speeches to the more credulous girls caused Mignon's stock to rise considerably higher. Others who knew her too well looked wise and held their peace. Mignon alone knew just how narrowly she had missed falling into a pit of Rowena's digging.

Quiet Constance entertained her own view of the incident. It coincided completely with Marjorie's thoughtful opinion. "It's hard to part a pair of girls like those two," she said. "They have too much in common. Between you and me, I don't imagine Mignon will stick to us very long. She's not interested in us."

"No, I suppose she thinks us rather too stiff-necked. Oh, well, we can only do our best and let the future take care of itself. There's the doorbell, Connie. That must be Jerry. She told Captain she'd come over early. Will you go down and escort her in state to my house?"

Constance vanished to return almost immediately, but without Jerry. She had not come back empty-handed, however. A large, white pasteboard box bearing the name "Braley's" revealed the fact that Hal had outstripped his sister.

"Oh, the gorgeous things!" gurgled Marjorie, as she lifted a great sheaf of long-stemmed pink rosebuds from the box. Her pale cheeks took color from the roses as she spied Hal's card with a cheering message written underneath in his flowing, boyish hand. "He's been such a comfort! Just as soon as I get well I'm going to have a little dance and invite all the boys." Marjorie touched the fragrant token with a friendly hand. "Laurie sent me some violets yesterday. Those on the chiffonier."

"He sent me some, too," admitted Constance rather shyly.

"How strange!" dimpled Marjorie. "Oh, there's the bell again! That surely must be Jerry!"

Before Constance was half way downstairs, Jerry was half way up, her broad face beaming, her arms laden with a large, round object, strangely resembling a cake.

"Oh, take it!" she gasped. "My arms are breaking."

Constance coming to her rescue, the two girls soon made haven with Marjorie and a lively chattering began. Frequent alarms at the front door denoted steadily arriving guests and a little past two found Marjorie's strictly informal reception in full swing, with girls tucked into every convenient corner of her room. Her own particular chums, including Ellen Seymour and Esther Lind, were all there. Even Susan and Muriel, who had been busy getting well while she lay ill, were able to be present. Lucy Warner was also among the happy throng, a trifle shy, but with a new look of gentleness in her green eyes and a glad little smile on her somber face.

Mignon appeared, but did not stay to the merry-making. She was full of polite sympathy and apparently bent on doing the agreeable. But in her black eyes lay a curious, furtive expression, which Marjorie mentally decided made her look more than ever like the Evil Genius. After a sojourn of perhaps twenty minutes, during which she walked about restlessly from girl to girl, exchanging commonplaces, she pleaded an engagement and took her leave.

Her presence somewhat of a strain, her departure was not mourned. Now wholly congenial, the party dropped all reserve and became exceedingly hilarious. Despite Mrs. Dean's protests, they had insisted on bringing their own refreshments, and later on Marjorie's pink-and-white house was turned into a veritable picnic ground. Jerry's weighty contribution turned out to be an immense many-layered cake, thickly iced and decorated. "A regular whale of a cake," she styled it, and no one contradicted her. After the luncheon had been eaten to the ceaseless buzz of girlish voices, each trying to out-talk the other, the company proceeded further to amuse the lovely convalescent with various funny little stunts at their command.

"Girls," at last reminded thoughtful Irma, "it is after four o'clock. We mustn't tire Marjorie out. I move we go downstairs to the living room and lift up our voices for her benefit in a good, old-fashioned song. Then we'll come back, say good-bye and run home."

The wisdom of Irma's proposal conceded, the singers trooped downstairs. Presently, through the open door, the sound of their clear, young voices came up to her as she lay back listening, a bright smile irradiating her delicate features. It was so beautiful to know that others cared so much about making her happy. She had so many things to be thankful for.

Afterward when all except Jerry and Constance had kissed her good-bye and departed with bubbling good wishes, she said soberly: "Girls, doesn't it make you positively shiver when you think that next year will be our last in Sanford High? After that we'll be scattered. Most of us are going away to college. That means we'll only see each other during vacations. I can't bear to think of it."

"Some of us will still be together," declared Jerry stoutly. "Susan, Muriel and I are going to Hamilton College if you do. You see, you can't lose us."

"I don't wish to lose you." Marjorie patted Jerry's hand. Her brown eyes rested a trifle wistfully on Constance. Marjorie knew, as did Jerry, that Connie intended to go to New York to study grand opera as soon as her high school life was over.

"You are thinking of Connie." Jerry's eyes had followed Marjorie's glance. "She won't be lost to us. Hamilton isn't so very far from New York. But what's the use in worrying when we've some of this year left yet and another year before us? One thing at a time is my motto."

"You are a philosopher, Jeremiah." Marjorie brightened. "'One thing at a time,'" she repeated. "That's the right idea. When I go back to school again, I'm going to try my hardest to make the rest of my junior year a success. I can't say much about my senior year. It's still an undiscovered territory. I'm just going to remember that it's a soldier's first duty to go where he's ordered and ask no questions. When I'm ordered to my senior year, all I can do is salute the colors and forward march!"

"Lead on and we'll follow," asserted Jerry Macy gallantly. "I guess we can hike along and leave a few landmarks on that precious senior territory. When I come into senior estate I shall use nothing but the most elegant English. As I am still a junior I can still say, 'Geraldine, Jerry, Jeremiah, you've got to beat it. It's almost five o'clock.'"

Left together, after Jerry had made extravagantly ridiculous farewells, Constance seated herself beside Marjorie's bed. "Are you tired, Lieutenant?" was her solicitous question.

"Not a bit. I'm going to make Captain let me go downstairs to-morrow. It's time I was up and doing again. I am way behind in my lessons."

"You'll catch up," comforted Constance. Inwardly she was reflecting that she doubted whether there were any situation with which Marjorie Dean could not catch up. Her feet were set in ways of light that wandered upward to the stars. Though to those who courted darkness it might appear that she sometimes faltered, Constance knew that those same steady feet would carry her unfalteringly through her senior year to the wider life to come.

How Marjorie explored her new senior territory and what landmarks she left behind in passing will be told in "Marjorie Dean, High School Senior."

THE END

Milton Keynes UK
Ingram Content Group UK Ltd.
UKHW022003250624
444714UK00010B/421

9 781836 573043